RAIN DANCE

Those who say
only the sun
brings happiness
have never
danced
in the rain.

Wisdom from the wall of the ladies' room at
Klondike Kate's, Dawson City, Yukon, July 2004

ACT I

ONE

"I WISH YOU HAD taken me dancing, Stan."

He didn't answer.

She dug the shovel back into the ground, scooping up another bite of soil.

Stan sat against the wall of the ditch, staring vacantly as the dirt landed with a soft *whump* on the growing pile.

Ellen's voice was quiet, wistful. "Once in a while a woman likes to do something a little different. Kick up her heels, get some exercise." *Whump.* "I guess digging is exercise, too. But dancing, well, that's a bit more sociable."

His eyes were glazed. *Typical Friday night,* she thought. *Come staggering home from Jugs, drunk half out of your mind and utterly useless.* "I suppose the usual crowd was there?" *Whump.* Still no response.

But then, she didn't really expect one.

"Reminds me of landscaping the yard, me with the

shovel and you on your butt. Course, there should be a beer in your hand." *Whump.* "Guess you've had your fill of that." She patted her hip pocket. "I'll check your wallet when I get home, but I'm betting we're broke again." *Whump.*

Leaning on the shovel, Ellen pulled off her cap and shook her short brown curls. She wiped her forehead with the back of one gloved hand and surveyed her work, forcing her eyes to focus. The nearest street lamp was almost a block away. Its dim light filtered through a stand of evergreens but didn't penetrate down below the broken pavement which, above her head, lined the rim of the freshly dug ditch. She may as well have been in a tunnel. *Like trench warfare, without the mud,* she thought, pausing to listen. *All quiet on the western front.*

She pushed the button on her watch. Three A.M. Wasn't there a song about this time of night? Something about being lonely. She filled her shovel again.

Lonely. *Whump.* Some romantic young songwriter's version of loneliness; nothing like the lonely you get from fourteen years of an empty marriage. *Whump.*

Light drops of rain caressed the back of her neck, and she turned up her face for a few seconds before heaving out the next scoop of dirt. *Whump.*

This valley was the closest thing to desert that Canada offered, and the dry climate suited her perfectly. But tonight, she had suddenly developed a sincere appreciation for rain.

Whump. The rain had brought her to this.

Well, the rain and Clarissa Simms.

With Stan about as conversational as ever, Ellen's mind wandered back a few hours to the afternoon, when Clarissa had reached for another cigarette, kicked off her sandals, and pressed her feet into the lawn. "Your grass needs a trim."

"That's next. Just have to finish this flower bed."

"You work too hard."

Ellen snipped the shriveled blossoms from the daffodils. "The sun's shining. It's pleasant work. And Monte likes the company." The border collie lifted his ears at the sound of his name, but he stayed curled up on the grass at Ellen's side. "How are your boys?"

Clarissa snorted. "Who knows? Dave hasn't let me speak to them all week." She flicked ash from the end of her cigarette.

"Still having trouble sorting out custody?"

"Yeah. This Mom's-week, Dad's-week thing is bull." Clarissa turned her chair so that her long brown legs caught the sun more evenly. "Being a widow has gotta be a whole lot easier. Wish I'd thought of that before I tossed Dave out. Too late now."

Whump. Ellen had been shocked. Clarissa was rather selfish, and more than a little bossy, but—violent? Her surprise must have shown on her face; Clarissa laughed, amused.

"Oh, yeah. I mean it. You know how he's deathly allergic to strawberries? Would've been too easy—just buy something tasty with strawberries listed in the fine print. Oopsie!"

Ellen sat back on her heels. "Clarissa, he's the father of your children."

"Yeah. And maybe he should have thought of them once in a while, instead of spending all his spare time chasing skirts." Clarissa exhaled. "This sudden need to be a daddy is a farce. Makes him look the real family man for little Miss-Martha-Wanna-be-Stewart." Leaning from the lounger, she crushed out her cigarette on the rock wall of Ellen's flower bed.

"He's still living with that one?" Ellen pulled up a dandelion.

"Yeah. He's such a sponge." Clarissa smiled. "Although I doubt she'll put up with my boys trashing her perfect little house much longer. Besides, I don't think Dave can keep up the good-daddy routine. Either way, she's bound to ditch him. Then he'll go back on the prowl, forget about the kids, and I'll be scrambling to line up sitters for my evening shifts." She stretched out again. "Trust me. Life's a whole lot easier if you're a widow."

"Thirty-three's too young to be widowed."

"Yeah? Well, it's too old for wasting time in a bad marriage."

Ellen sighed. She knew where this was headed.

"Really, El. Thirty-three's young. You're in decent shape. Maybe a bit short, but you're not hard to look at. Hell, you'd be damn pretty if you'd put on some make-up. Do something with your hair. Guys would be all over you."

"That's enough of that." Ellen stood and gathered her tools. "Want to stay for supper?"

Clarissa shifted in the lounger, looked at her painted toenails. "Uh, thanks. No. I've got stuff to do."

"You have to eat."

"Yeah. I'm fine, really. Some other time." Clarissa slid her feet back into her sandals. "Actually, I should wander on home now. Thanks for the offer, though." She closed the gate, waved from the sidewalk, and was gone.

Folding the lounger, Ellen recoiled from Clarissa's special combination of heavy floral perfume laced with cigarettes.

Her nose had always been hypersensitive.

Whump.

Stan stunk. Beer and cigarettes. She could smell him from here. Standing on the pile of dirt, she put her gloved hands on the broken pavement and pulled herself up to look over the rim of the ditch. In the distance, beyond the hulk of a crane and a huge cylinder of concrete, a lone car crossed the intersection of Government and York.

The rain was just a drizzle. The forecast had called for this: overcast skies, clearing by morning. Ellen climbed down from the pile and used the shovel as a measuring stick. It came to a couple of inches under her chin, so what would that be... maybe four feet? That meant the hole in the bottom of the ditch would be what, about two and a half feet wide, six long, and—she tilted the handle into the hole—a couple of feet deep.

Perfect. Good thing Stan hadn't been genetically disposed to fat. All those years on a bar stool at Jugs hadn't amounted to much; a few pounds of beer belly on an otherwise scrawny frame.

She checked over the rim of the ditch again, rehearsing the hastily-composed script of her contingency plan: "Oh, my, this is *so* embarrassing. My husband seems to have fallen into this ditch and passed out. I've been piling up dirt so I could hoist him out, but I just don't know how I'll manage. So embarrassing to *call* anyone, especially at this hour of the night, but since you're *here*..."

Not a soul in sight.

"Well, Stan, it's been a slice." She took him by the boots and heaved him away from the wall. His head slid down the wall of the ditch and dragged along in the dirt, carving a small ditch of its own.

Ellen dropped his feet and stepped into the hole. Reaching across his torso, she grasped his arm and hip and rolled him toward her, settling him into the three-quarter prone position the instructors had taught her in first-aid class. *Prevents choking if patient vomits while unconscious.*

Stepping out of the hole, she moved behind him. A small push, and he settled gently into place.

Above the ditch, all was quiet. She smiled, mentally feeding the contingency-plan speech through a shredder. Then, working as quickly and quietly as possible, she pushed dirt back into the hole, spreading the pile until the bottom of the ditch was as smooth as the city workers had left it.

She moved to the downhill side of the ditch. At about knee-height the open end of a broad concrete pipe penetrated the wall. Stooping, she reached in and pulled out her gardening jacket. Walking backwards to the uphill end of the ditch, she swept the jacket from side to side, scuffing out her boot-marks. Not that anyone was likely to notice. Still, no point leaving anything behind that would show anyone had been there.

Ellen straightened and leaned her shovel against the wall, squinting through the dark. A second concrete pipe protruded several feet into the ditch at this end, about waist-height. She set her jacket in its opening. Balancing with one foot on the jacket, she climbed up onto the top of the pipe. Lying on her belly she reached down and retrieved her jacket, flicking out the dirt left by her boot. She crawled along the pipe to the end of the ditch and stood up to look out over the pavement. When she was sure she was alone, she pulled herself out of the ditch, then reached for the shovel and hauled it up.

Unbuckling one strap of her overalls, she slid the handle of the shovel down into her pant leg and settled its end into her boot. The blade nestled cold and hard against her breast. As she stowed her gloves, her fingers brushed the wallet. She had a moment of doubt.

Maybe she should have left it with him.

No. Better this way. In the unlikely event that he was found, robbery would be the natural motive. *Poor guy musta got rolled on his way home from the bar. Prob'ly never knew what hit 'im.*

Rain dripped gently from the evergreens. She pulled her cap low, buttoned her jacket and walked home, limping slightly as the shovel thumped against her knee.

WHEN ELLEN'S ALARM WENT OFF at 7:00 she was already outside, poking about in the cool dirt of the rose bed. As forecast, the cloud cover had burned off; the day promised to be warm and sunny.

The earth smelled fresh from the rain. Ellen sat back on her heels, breathing deeply. She loved spring. It was the time of new beginnings.

Opening the back door, she leaned into the house and

took Monte's leash from its hook. Monte, quivering with excitement, sat obediently until he heard the snap of the clasp. Then he lunged toward the gate. "Wait, Monte. Let me lock up."

She patted her pocket. The lump of keys bulged in its customary place. Flicking up the button on the inside of the lock, she pulled the door closed behind her.

On Government, heavy equipment had already roared to life. Monte shuddered and skulked at the end of his leash, straining away from the noise. As they passed, Ellen watched the crane lift a huge concrete cylinder and lower it into the ditch, setting it on end with the openings in its sides facing the pipes. Monte pulled her toward the park, staring intently at the gulls that dotted the lawn. Herding instincts bred into his genes for generations snapped to attention. He quivered in anticipation.

Ellen tugged gently at his leash. "Come on. Let's see if Clarissa's outside for her morning smoke."

They headed down the alley, and Monte turned at the familiar back gate. Ellen's nose told her they would find the wooden chairs in the little ivy-covered arbor empty. Monte looked up at her. "Out late last night, I suspect."

By the time they were on their way back, the crane was lowering a length of concrete connecting pipe. It thunked reassuringly into place on the bottom of the ditch.

Monte cringed and pulled her toward home.

ELLEN CLOSED THE GATE AND REMOVED Monte's leash. Unlocking the back door, she tossed the dog a treat. "Good boy, Monte. You stay outside for a while."

In the bathroom, she flushed the toilet one more time. It seemed to be working fine.

Stan's wallet hadn't contained anything of value. Well, not to her. The wad of business cards had been valuable to Stan; he'd lovingly collected them over his years at Jugs.

Once, long ago, she'd summoned all her courage and

entered the smoky strip club, determined to leave with enough money to make the car payment on time. She had stood near the door, poised for flight, her eyes desperately sweeping the room for Stan. There he was, accepting a card from a man in a rumpled suit.

Hesitantly approaching, she had watched him look at the card, purse his lips and then nod, like a jeweler appraising a rare piece. Evidently, it was worthy: he opened his wallet and added it deliberately to his collection, placing it carefully within the pack. He pulled out a twenty, raised it in the air, and turned toward the bar. "One more for my friend here."

Ellen had turned and fled. She had been close enough to see that she was too late for the car payment. The twenty was all there was in his wallet. Well, aside from the card collection. This morning, their shredded remains had been added to one cup of water and ground to a paste in the food processor, then distributed to rot in the soil of the rose bed.

The plastic had required a different solution.

Rotary cutters, she thought, *have so many uses.*

Heck, she could write an infomercial: *"Slice through leather and plastic in no time!"* The camera would start with a close-up. In her deft hands, the wallet, driver's license, and debit card form neat, narrow strips on the cutting board. Quick ninety-degree turn of the board, a few more rapid slices, and the strips become minuscule squares. The camera zooms back from the cutting board, taking in Ellen's gingham apron, perfect hair and smiling face.

The tiny pieces of plastic and leather had flushed without any trouble, and so far nothing had resurfaced into the bowl.

Of course there had been no money. What hadn't gone for beer would have ended up in the pull-tab machines. A quick check with internet banking gave the balance of his account: $2.58. Ellen had started her own separate account a few years ago, desperate to save the house. The car was long gone.

The phone rang. She checked her watch: 7:40. Call display confirmed it was the factory.

"Stan there?" Male voice, impatient.

"I'm sorry, he's at work. Can I take a message?"

"I'm *calling* from PenWest. Stan hasn't shown up yet."

Ellen feigned surprise. "That's odd. He left ages ago, before I woke up."

The foreman snorted. "This'll be the third time this month. Tell him if he isn't here in fifteen minutes, he can look for another job." He didn't wait for a reply.

Smiling, Ellen hung up the phone.

When she had showered and changed for work, Ellen filled Monte's dish with fresh water and set it outside. "Mind the fort, boy." She flicked the lock on the back door, gave Monte a final pat, closed the gate that separated the back yard from the front, and walked to the bus stop.

As her bus made its way down Government, traffic slowed to a crawl. Under the evergreens, a dump truck tilted its load into the ditch, covering the new concrete pipes that connected the last cylinder to the rest of the storm sewer network.

WORK WAS UNEVENTFUL, and the afternoon sun was still warm when she walked from the office to the bus stop. Traffic was held up again on the way home. This time a truck was dumping asphalt; its acrid smell stung her eyes, and she smiled.

Monte danced with excitement when he heard her coming up the lane. "How's my boy? Ready for a walk?" She let him into the porch and headed to the bedroom to change. Odd, she thought as she opened the blinds. Usually she opened them right after she made the bed. But then, it hadn't exactly been a typical morning. She pulled on jeans and a t-shirt, shoved her feet into her sandals, and grabbed the leash.

Monte lowered his ears as they passed the steamroller.

They crossed the park, headed up the alley. Clarissa's chair was still empty, and Ellen knocked on her back door. She stooped and let Monte off his leash. No answer. Monte ran to the arbor and returned with a battered flying disc in his mouth. Ellen tossed it, then turned back to the door. She tried the handle: locked.

Monte had taken the disc back to the arbor and now sat beside the chairs, waiting expectantly. Ellen laughed, settling into one of the chairs. "Here boy." She tossed the disc, then leaned over to deadhead a couple of flowers. Clarissa's yard was beautiful in an untamed way, prickly here and there with unexpected thorns; Ellen's yard was tidy, its beds orderly, its thorns safely confined.

Monte dropped the disc on the empty chair and looked at Ellen.

"I know, boy. That's twice today we've missed her." Ellen rubbed his ears. Most days, during walk time, Clarissa and Ellen would share a quick visit, Monte and Ellen quenching their thirst while Clarissa got her daily fix of nicotine, stubbing her cigarettes in the heavy glass bowl of an antique stand-up ashtray. Ellen had long coveted the ashtray, thinking it would make a fabulous plant stand.

Ellen pointed. "Look, Monte. No ashtray. Maybe she quit." Monte cocked his head, perking his ears. His tail thumped.

"Yes, I suppose it's time to go."

On Government, the paving crew was finished; smooth, black asphalt stretched under the evergreens.

Ellen closed the back gate and released Monte. She opened the gate to the front yard. "Get the paper, Monte." He bounded around the house but didn't return. She followed and found him staring up at the mailbox. The paper was inside, out of his reach. "Poor Monte," she said, reaching down to pat his head as she pulled the paper from the box. "Here. You carry it around back."

Straightening up, she stopped. Stan's keys dangled from the front door.

Well, that explained why they weren't on him last night. Wondering how long they'd been there, she put them in her pocket. This wasn't the first time he'd left his keys in the lock. Responsibility had never been his strong suit. Nor had cooperation; evidently, he had preferred to use the front door. Small wonder the living room always seemed to need vacuuming.

As of today, her housework had probably been cut in half.

She tossed Monte a treat and flipped open the paper, scanning the headlines. *LET IT RAIN! Storm Drain Project Finished Today*. Smiling, she unlocked the back door.

The message light was flashing: PenWest. Stan hadn't shown up for work at all. Ellen stifled a giggle. Really, she thought. If he had shown up today, they wouldn't have liked it much.

Dialing, she feigned concern. "Hello. You called about my husband, Stan. ... No, I just got home myself. ... That's funny. He left before I got up this mor— " She gasped. "Yes. Yes, I'm still here. I just realized, he... he might not have come home last night.... No, I... I'm sorry. I'll have to get back to you. I really don't know what's going on."

She hung up the phone and dialed Jugs.

"Hello. I wonder if I could speak to someone who was working last night? ... You were? Could you please tell me if Stan Hoskins was in there last night? ... Yes.... Are you sure? ... Well, thank you anyway."

Slowly, she hung up the phone.

Stan hadn't been at Jugs for over a week.

Well, then, where *had* he gone?

Ellen went into her office. Bending under the computer desk, she pressed the button of the power bar. As she straightened, her nose wrinkled.

She turned, sniffing. What was that smell? It was out-of-place, yet familiar. Heavy, floral. She turned her head again, trying to catch the scent. On the windowsill, the afternoon sun lit up a vase of wilting hyacinths. She sniffed. Not quite, but... well, maybe. She took it into the kitchen, dropped the flowers into the compost and set the vase by the sink. A short beep from the office announced that the computer was ready.

Logging on to the bank's website, she clicked on Stan's account and scrolled through his transactions, checking yesterday's entries. Two withdrawals. The first, for $150, was at 9:24 P.M., long after she had dished his supper into containers. That was, she mused, about the time she had realized that he wasn't going to be taking her out dancing, and that this anniversary would, like those before it, pass unnoticed.

The last withdrawal, for $20, was at 12:03 A.M. She had still been awake, tossing restlessly as the night grew ever more oppressive in anticipation of a storm that never did materialize, Clarissa's words reverberating through her head, feeding the swollen, throbbing disappointment until it suddenly metamorphosized into an unfamiliar rage. Ellen recalled with a curious sense of detachment the seething fury that exploded and then just as quickly cooled—not into calm acceptance but into an icy cold that burned with its own intensity. She had risen, filled with firm and deadly resolve, dressed, and left the house, leaving the bewildered Monte and taking instead the shovel from against the garden shed. Tucking it under her jacket she had walked toward the shadows of the evergreens lining Government Street, to patiently await Stan's final staggering journey home from Jugs. Except that he hadn't been to Jugs.

Well, Ellen thought, dialing the non-emergency number for the police. Now I don't have to pretend I'm confused.

The officer who responded to her call seemed unconcerned. After all, Mr. Hoskins had only been gone twenty-four hours. Had she checked the hospitals? Any medical conditions they should know about? Drug use?

Bank information couldn't be followed up on until Monday. They'd look into it. In the meantime, she should try not to worry. Stan would no doubt show up. So she waited.

THE AFTERNOON SUN glinted off Constable Harland's badge. Twin beams reflected like headlights from his dark glasses, and she was relieved when he removed them. His eyes were concerned, but professional.

Peeling off her gardening gloves, Ellen quieted Monte with a pat on the head. She looked up at the officer.

The cash withdrawals hadn't been made at Jugs. The first was from a machine in a cozy little dinner-and-dance bistro over in Westside, the second at the gas station in Summerland.

Harland consulted his notes. "Night clerk at the gas station says he remembers a couple that came through around midnight. The woman was driving. She pumped the gas while the guy sat in the car. She used *his* bank card to pull cash out of the machine—refused to pay through the till with it—and she made two trips back to the car for the guy's PIN code. Apparently the guy was..." his finger traced his notes "... too drunk to be useful."

Flipping the page, he continued. "Clerk thought she was acting kind of nervous. Plus she seemed a little drunk herself, and he thought maybe he should call the cops, so he wrote down their license number. Car's registered to a woman—lives a couple blocks from here, just off Government. I'm heading there to question her."

He glanced at her over his notebook. "Ever heard of a Clarissa Simms?"

TWO

ELLEN'S BREATH RUSHED out of her chest. Under her hand, Monte's head tilted up. He whimpered softly.

"It's okay, boy," she said automatically, stroking his ears. She felt the officer's eyes on her, and she steadied herself to meet his gaze.

"Clarissa. Yes. She's a friend of mine." How cool she sounded; how normal. She shook her head.

Harland seemed to think he understood. "Don't worry, ma'am. I'm sure they'll have a perfectly reasonable explanation."

Ellen held his gaze. "I'm sure they will."

Harland shifted his weight. He looked from her face down to Monte, then up to his notebook. He shifted again, snapped the notebook shut, and reached for his dark glasses. By the time he had them in place, Ellen had bent to pick up Monte's ball. She could still feel Harland watching her. She tossed the ball, and Monte obliged by loping after it.

"Does Ms. Simms know?"

His question startled her. "Know what?"

"Does she know that your husband is... missing."

"Oh." Ellen paused. "No, I guess she doesn't."

The officer's eyebrows rose behind his glasses.

"She's not a close friend?"

"Close?" Ellen repeated. What was he getting at?

Harland tilted his head. "You haven't spoken to her?"

"Not for a couple of days, now, no."

"You didn't call to tell her about your husband?"

Monte dropped his ball at Ellen's feet and looked up at her, expectant.

"I'm a very private person, Constable Harland." She bent for the ball, tossed it again, watched Monte chase it. "I don't see any reason to let people know that my husband hasn't bothered to come home."

Again his eyebrows appeared over the tops of his glasses. "And yet you called us."

Ellen raised her shoulders. "I thought I should."

Harland flipped open his notebook, but didn't look at it. "He ever done this before?"

Ellen dropped her hand to Monte's head. "Done what?"

"Not come home." Harland waited.

"No." Ellen thought for a moment, shook her head. "No, he's always come home."

Harland finally looked down at his notebook. He clicked his pen.

"You two have a fight?"

"A fight?"

"Yeah. You know, a quarrel? An argument? He complain about supper, forget your anniversary, something like that?"

Ellen considered this. "No." She stooped for the ball, tossed it. "No, we didn't have a fight."

Harland removed his glasses again, stared down at her. "Excuse me for saying this, ma'am, but you don't seem awful concerned."

"Concerned?"

He snapped the notebook shut again. "Yeah, concerned. You called us, remember? You said your husband had been missing since Friday night. Said he should have been home, but he wasn't." Now Harland's brows knitted into a frown. "Yet you don't seem worried at all. You want us to look for him?"

Ellen drew herself up. "Of course." She looked Harland square in the face. "Of course I want you to look for him. I *was* worried about him. But you told me yourself he'd been out with Clarissa at a dance club, and that she drove him home." Clarissa. This was an unexpected betrayal. Her mouth was suddenly dry, her voice tight. "Maybe he's still there. With her."

Did that sound right? A good combination of hurt and confusion, with just a tad of indignation? She waited.

Harland replaced his glasses. "Alright, ma'am. Guess there's no point calling out Search and Rescue until we've heard what Ms. Simms has to say."

Ellen's mind raced. "You'll let me know? If he's... with her or... not?" There. She really was getting emotional now, raw nerves too near the surface. Harland was plainly relieved. John Wayne rescues damsel in distress: this role he understood, this he could handle. She half expected him to say "Whal, doncha worry, li'l lady. Ah'll find yer husband fer ya."

The dark glasses came back off. "Don't worry, ma'am. I'll find your husband for you."

A snort of hysterical laughter escaped. Ellen was relieved when Constable Harland responded considerately, as though she was choking back tears.

ELLEN CRUMPLED ONTO THE STEP, twining her fingers into Monte's fur. She buried her face in his neck as the police car pulled away from the curb. Monte turned and gave her a playful lick.

"Oh, Monte." With the back of her hand she wiped one eye, then the other. She lowered her head until her forehead touched her knees. Monte whimpered as her mood dropped.

"Monte boy. What is going on?"

He waited patiently at her feet.

"Clarissa." Ellen reached over to rub his ears. Wooden chairs in the arbor, empty since Friday night. "Stan and Clarissa." Suddenly, her head was reeling. A wave of nausea flooded over her, and she scrambled unsteadily to her feet. She reached for the doorknob. Locked. Crap. She patted her pockets for keys.

Faster to run to the back door. She bolted around the house, through the door. Too far to the bathroom.

Damn.

She emptied her stomach into the kitchen sink.

Great. Just great. She crumpled to the floor with her cheek against the cool tile of the floor. Obedient as always, Monte stayed in the porch, whimpering with concern.

She sat up. "I'm okay, Monte. It's alright." She rested her head against her knees for a moment, waiting for the room to stop spinning, then pulled herself up.

She started to clean the sink. "Damn." Bile rose again, and she fled to the bathroom. This time, she made it.

She pulled the cleanser from under the sink and returned to the kitchen. Holding her breath, she squirted the sink, grabbed a handful of paper towel and started scrubbing, trying to breathe through her mouth, trying to pretend she didn't already know what it smelled like. She threw the soiled paper towel in the garbage, sprayed the sink again, and grabbed another handful of towels.

That smell. She fought the urge to vomit. *Think about something else.* She forced her thoughts away from her actions, and her mind skipped and flitted.

Rain.

No.

Flowers, bobbing, rain, fresh scent of… no, no. Something else. Not smells.

News. What's in the news. Newspaper. Storm drain… no.

Break-ins up. Theft from autos up. Keep your doors locked, valuables out of cars, out of sight…

Locked.

Stan's keys had been in the door.

Slowly, Ellen rinsed the sink, then pumped soap onto her hands and scrubbed them. Its floral scent usually annoyed her, but today it would help fight the smell of vomit. She rinsed her hands.

Her eyes fell on the empty vase.

That smell. Floral. Heavy.

Not decaying hyacinths. Clarissa.

Stan's keys had been in the door. And Clarissa had been in the office.

Ellen leaned against the sink.

Clarissa? In the office? Why?

Don't be silly, Ellen. She shook her head. You can't be sure.

The front of her shirt was wet. She pushed herself away from the sink, headed for the bedroom. Pulling a clean shirt from the drawer, she reached to close the blinds.

Close the blinds.

She sank to the bed. The blinds had been closed that day. The keys had been in the door. Clarissa had been in her office.

Why?

On the street, a car slowed to a stop. Monte gave a low woof as the engine silenced. A door slammed.

Ellen pulled herself upright as footsteps approached the house. Monte woofed another warning, then barked as the doorbell rang.

"Thanks, Monte. It's alright." She unlocked the door.

Constable Harland stood on the front step, notebook in hand. His head tilted briefly. "Ma'am."

He removed his glasses, and she realized he was being careful not to stare at her shirt. She looked down at the wet stain, dismayed to see flecks of vomit.

Harland was watching her with sympathy. "Excuse me a moment," she said.

"Of course."

Ellen left him standing on the steps, and quickly changed her shirt. Stopping at the bathroom, she rinsed her face, then swished a bit of mouthwash and spat.

"Sorry." She closed the door behind her and stood on the front porch, facing him.

"That's alright, ma'am." Harland indicated the porch chair, all sympathy now. "You've had a shock."

"I'm alright." Ellen remained standing.

Harland flipped open his notebook. "Well. Ms. Simms was home. She says yes, she drove your husband home on Friday night. Says she found him at the Blue Moon, over in Westside. He was pretty drunk and the manager wanted him out of there. So she gave him a ride."

Ellen considered this. "Was she... was she there *with* him?"

"Not according to her. She says she met a date there, some guy from Kelowna. We'll be checking up on that. Says she just gave Mr. Hoskins a ride home, that's all."

Ellen realized she had been holding taut every muscle in her body. As some of the tension left her back, her legs started to shake.

Harland looked concerned. "Why don't you sit, ma'am."

She sagged into the porch chair. Her head was spinning again, and she leaned forward to rest it on her knees.

"You alright?"

Ellen raised her head. "Yes, yes I'm fine." She met his eyes. "Constable Harland, where are my manners. Would you like a glass of lemonade, iced tea?"

"No thanks, ma'am. I'd like to follow up on some of this." He tapped his notebook. "Can I call someone?"

"No, no. I'm fine."

Harland nodded, all fatherly consideration now. Ellen pictured him back at the office, giving his report. *Tough li'l lady, this one.*

She straightened her back, and he smiled again. "Alright, then. I'll be talking to the folks at the Blue Moon, and the guy from Kelowna. I'll let you know what I find out."

"Thank you." She watched him turn to leave. This time he didn't put his dark glasses back on until he reached the car.

So Clarissa had been meeting a dinner date that evening. Ellen's thoughts drifted back to Friday afternoon. She hadn't really meant to ask Clarissa to supper; at the time, she'd still harbored a flimsy notion that she and Stan could manage some sort of anniversary celebration. The dinner invitation had popped out automatically, so she'd been relieved at Clarissa's quick turn-down. Did she have a new lover she didn't want to discuss?

Was that lover Stan?

"Ellen?"

She raised her head, startled. Clarissa was on the sidewalk, a brown paper bag in her hand.

"Clarissa." Behind her, in the house, Monte gave a short woof.

Clarissa approached. "You... okay?"

Ellen stood. "I'm alright. Come in." She held the door open.

Clarissa went in ahead of her. She seemed a stranger in familiar surroundings. Hesitantly, she pulled off her shoes and picked them up, heading for the kitchen. In the back porch, Monte wagged his tail in welcome. Clarissa set down her shoes and patted his head. "Hello, boy."

"Tea?" Ellen stood at the sink, kettle in hand.

"I brought supplies." Clarissa opened the bag and pulled out a bottle of Amaretto. "No Grand Marnier, sorry."

"So." Ellen set two mugs on the table, leaned her back against the counter. "Tell me about Friday."

Clarissa squirmed in her chair, drummed her red nails on the table top. "Friday." She met Ellen's gaze for a moment, then looked away. "Yes, well. Friday..." She stared out the window. Her gaze flicked back toward Ellen. She put both palms flat on the table. "Damn it, El—"

Monte's collar rattled as his head jerked upright, alert.

Clarissa took a breath and started over. "Look, I'm sorry I didn't tell you. I should have. Actually, I tried." She sat back in her chair, looked Ellen square in the face. "I was afraid you'd shoot the messenger."

Behind Ellen, the kettle shrieked.

Clicked.

Sighed into silence.

She turned, made the tea. Carrying the pot to the table, she pulled out a chair and sat. "Okay. I won't shoot you." She pushed a mug across the table. "Tell me what happened."

Clarissa opened the Amaretto, poured a shot into her mug, and passed the bottle to Ellen. "I was at the Blue Moon. There was this guy."

Ellen returned the bottle, and their eyes met. Clarissa shrugged. "You wouldn't approve, so I didn't tell you."

"Wouldn't approve?" Ellen poured tea into both mugs. "Why wouldn't I approve?"

"Internet date." Clarissa put the top back on the Amaretto. "Didn't work out anyway." She sipped her tea.

Ellen waited.

Clarissa set her mug down. "Ellen, Stan was there with a woman."

"A woman?"

"Of course, with a woman. Why else would he be at the Blue Moon. If he was out with the guys, he'd have been at Jugs, or Lucille's. He was with a woman."

Ellen nodded. "Of course he was with a woman."

Clarissa gave a snort of exasperation. "Then why..." She stopped. Her eyes widened, then narrowed. "Ellen, you didn't."

"Didn't what?" Ellen felt the color creeping up her neck.

"You thought *I* was there *with* Stan?" Clarissa demanded, incredulous. "Ellen, I hate to break it to you, but Stan is about the last guy I'd go out with." She bit her lip. "Sorry. That sounded... God." She groaned, closing her eyes.

Ellen sipped her tea, staring out of the window. "I know he's no catch." She'd always known that on some level. She knew it before the first time he hit her, before he hurt Monte. She looked across the table. "So. Who was he with?"

Clarissa groaned again. "Some little slut. Could have been a hooker, maybe a stripper. Probably both. Sleazy little thing."

"How come you brought him home?"

Clarissa stifled a smile. "She ditched him there."

"Ditched him?"

"Yeah. She was kissy-face all over him until he got back from the cash machine. Then she was out of there like a shot with some biker that had been in there all along. And Stan's cash."

My cash, thought Ellen.

"Ellen, you know his temper." She glanced at the small white scar on Ellen's temple. "He started cussing, kicking chairs around. Manager wanted him gone."

"So you drove him home."

"Yeah. My date was a bust anyway. Lousy conversation during supper, and he stiffed me with the drink bill, ran me out of cash. I had to use Stan's card to buy gas on the way home."

Ellen took another sip of tea. "Constable Harland said you'd paid for it with Stan's card. How come he stayed in the car?"

Clarissa shook her head. "He was drunk when we left the bar, but he seemed to get a whole lot worse on the way home. Like he and that tramp had maybe done some... Well. He was being weird." She looked at Ellen, then away. Finally, she faced her. "Look, Ellen. I don't... I..." Her long nails swept the table top, traced the edges. She took a breath, and finally blurted it out. "He was trying to grope me on the way home."

Ellen swallowed hard.

"I'm sorry." Clarissa shook her head. "I really didn't want to tell you."

Ellen stared, unseeing, out the window. "Has he done that before?"

"Groped me? No!" Clarissa took another sip of tea. "Look, Ellen, I'm sorry. You should know that Stan's been cheating on you. But my God, not with me."

Ellen watched a fly walk across the window pane. Outside, a bee hovered under the eaves for a moment, then lazily wandered off. The clock ticked, deafening in the stillness. She covered her ears.

Clarissa reached across the table and put her hand on Ellen's arm. "I'm sorry," she said again.

Ellen uncovered her ears and took Clarissa's hand in both of hers. "Where did you take him?"

"What?"

"Where did you leave Stan, on Friday night?" Ellen squeezed Clarissa's hand, then let go. "You said you brought him home, Clarissa. Your home, or here?"

"Oh." Clarissa raised her eyebrows. "Actually, neither."

"Neither?"

"No. He was groping me, pissing me off. When we were stopped for a red light at Main Street, I kicked him out of the car. Figured the walk home would do him good." Clarissa frowned. "I guess that was a bad idea. He never made it home?"

The fly was crawling up the curtains.

Ellen was intrigued by the question. Hadn't Harland told her? She watched the fly work its way across the curtain and onto the wall. "So. Tell me about Saturday."

THREE

CLARISSA SWALLOWED the last of her tea. She set her mug down. "Saturday?" she repeated.

Ellen looked at her. "Yes. Saturday."

"You were at work."

Ellen raised her eyebrows. "I always work Saturdays."

Clarissa reached for the bottle, poured herself another shot. She tipped the bottle toward Ellen, who nodded.

Ellen poured tea into both mugs. She set the teapot down.

"You were here."

Clarissa took a deep breath. "I shouldn't have let myself in, I know." She reached for her cigarettes, realized where she was, clasped her hands in front of her.

Ellen sipped her tea. "Clarissa, you have keys to my house. I trust you to water the plants, look after Monte if I can't." Monte's tail thumped at the sound of his name.

Clarissa squirmed. "This was different."

Ellen waited.

"I tried to check your email."

"My email?"

"Yeah." Clarissa drummed her nails against the table top. "You haven't checked it in days, have you?"

Ellen shook her head.

"I was still really angry with Stan when I got home. I was fed up with the way he treats you. I forgot it was none of my business, and I sent you an email, dishing the dirt on him and that tramp." Her cheeks flushed red. "Of course, in the morning I regretted it. It was none of my business, and a lousy way for you to find out. I couldn't face you. I expected you to call any moment. Finally, I clued in to the fact that you were at work. I figured I'd just come over and delete the email. You wouldn't have to know about it."

"Did you?"

"I came over and let myself in. But I couldn't figure out your password."

"So then what?"

"I..." Clarissa's blush deepened. "I heard you in the yard, talking to Monte, and I didn't want you to catch me in the house. It seemed so... so sneaky. So wrong." She took another swallow of tea. "I snuck out the front door."

"You left Stan's keys in the lock."

"What?"

"Stan's keys. You left them hanging in the lock."

Puzzled, Clarissa shook her head. "I used my own keys when I came in, at the back door. I just unlocked the dead-bolt on the front door and let myself out."

Ellen frowned.

"You were coming in through the back," Clarissa said. "I just pulled the door closed behind me and ran."

"Oh." Ellen traced the rim of her mug with the tip of her finger.

"Stan's keys were in the door?"

"Was that all you did while you were in the house?"

"Yes. Well, I gave Monte a treat when I got here."

"You weren't in the bedroom?"

"The *bedroom*?" Clarissa scowled. "Look, Ellen, I know how it must seem. That cute cop of yours thought I was tramping with Stan. I get that. But you've known me for years. What the hell would I be doing in your bedroom?"

Ellen sighed. "Nothing, Clarissa. It's just… nothing."

"Look, what is going on? Constable what's-his-name wouldn't really tell me anything. Is Stan gone, or what?"

Ellen leaned her elbows on the table and put her face in her hands. "I don't really know what's going on, Clarissa." She straightened, ran her hands over her hair. "Stan didn't come home Friday night."

"Well, what does he have to say about that?"

"Nothing." Ellen looked at her. "He hasn't been home since."

Clarissa whistled, low, then swore under her breath. "No kidding," she said. "Why didn't you call me? You must have been beside yourself with worry."

Worry? Ellen smiled faintly. Saturday and Sunday had been the most peaceful two days she'd had in a decade. No worries until today.

"I would have told you, if I'd seen you."

"Oh. Yeah." Clarissa poured another round of drinks. "Where do you think he is?"

Ellen shrugged. "You know, Clarissa, part of me just doesn't care."

"Well, yeah. I can see that, with Stan being such a prize and all. But still. What if he never turns up? Will you be okay?"

Ellen almost laughed. "I'll be fine."

"I mean financially and all that."

"Stan always spent more than he made."

"Oh." Clarissa frowned. "Ellen, don't tell the cops that."

Ellen looked at her, smiled. "Tell them what, that Stan was a useless jerk and I'm better off without him? No, I guess I hadn't ought to do that." She sipped her tea. "You were the last one seen with him. Better not tell them what you thought of him, either."

Clarissa made a face. "I already told the cop I didn't think much of Stan. I wasn't real blunt or anything. That cop… he's a hunk, eh?"

Ellen raised her eyebrows. "Is he?"

"Yeah. Didn't he remind you of some old cowboy, all strong and protective?"

Ellen smiled. "John Wayne."

"Yeah," Clarissa agreed. "A real old-fashioned good guy. When he wasn't wearing those stupid dark glasses. Make you feel like a bug under a microscope, or what?"

"So, you were out on an internet date."

"Yeah." Clarissa sighed. "Guy sounded nice on the phone. Bit of a jerk, though." She looked at Ellen. "Hey. If Stan doesn't come back, you wanna go on a manhunt with me?"

"You want us to look for him?"

Clarissa scowled. "I wouldn't spend any time hunting for Stan. Maybe to shoot him. Just kidding. No. I said a manhunt. There's gotta be a few good men left in this town. What's the scoop on that cop? Think he's married?"

Ellen laughed. Out in the porch, Monte finally relaxed.

ELLEN HUNG UP MONTE'S LEASH and tossed him a treat. They had taken the scenic route after walking Clarissa home, and now that the Amaretto had worn off Ellen was thinking a bit more clearly.

She checked the phone. No messages. While she waited for the computer to warm up, she put on a fresh pot of tea.

Settling at the computer, she checked her email. Three new messages. One on Thursday afternoon—the usual fare from an acquaintance back east, it was preceded by a string of forwards and no doubt followed by instructions to "pass it on." She deleted it. The second had been sent at 1:14 A.M., early Saturday morning, from Clarissa. Ellen smiled as she read the string of expletives Clarissa had used to describe Stan. No wonder she had wanted to retrieve it. She paused, re-read the last line. *You should get rid of that jerk. Hell, I'd be happy to do it for you.* Ellen printed it out, then deleted it.

The third was sent Saturday evening, at 7:02. She didn't recognize the sender's address. Glancing at the subject line, she froze. *i saw what u did.*

She stared at the screen.

What was this? She looked again at the address: IwatchU145@gmail.com. She moved the cursor over the message. Should she open it? Probably some kind of hoax, a virus. No, she shouldn't open it. She should delete it and then empty her trash folder.

i saw what u did.

She clicked on the message.

u should always keep your blinds closed mrs hoskins. always.

Ellen glanced up at the blinds. They *were* closed. Monte whimpered from the porch, and she jumped. It was nothing. Just the little snuffling noises he made in his sleep. *You're being silly,* she thought. She stared at the screen. ... *blinds closed ... blinds closed ... blinds closed. You should always keep your blinds closed.*

Stop this. She clicked delete, shut down the computer. As she bent to turn off the power bar, the doorbell rang. She jumped, heart in her throat. Startled from his sleep, Monte erupted into a frenzy of barking. Ellen sat frozen as the doorbell rang again.

"Mrs. Hoskins?"

Monte had stopped barking, but stood alert. "Come," said Ellen. He ventured past the porch. Clasping his collar firmly, Ellen approached the door.

"Who is it?"

"Constable Harland, ma'am. Sorry to come by so late, but I wanted to talk to you before I go off shift."

Ellen sighed, relaxing her hold on Monte's collar. "Good boy," she told him as he trotted to the back of the house.

Ellen opened the door. "Come in, please. Would you like to sit down?"

"Thanks, ma'am. I won't be but a minute. I called from

the office but I guess you were out. Didn't want to leave this on your answering machine. Thought I might catch you on my way home." Standing just inside the doorway, he flipped open his notebook.

"Well, I made some calls. Your friend's story checks out pretty good. She met another fellow at the Blue Moon, and Mr. Hoskins was there with another lady. Sorry." He glanced at her over his notebook. "Bad news, that one, according to the staff. She's in there a lot. Usually comes in with a new guy, but always leaves with the same biker."

Ellen took a moment to absorb this. "You mean, her... her pimp?"

"We're looking into it. They're running some kind of scam."

Great, Ellen thought. Well, if the police have to stay involved, it's good they're looking in some other direction.

"That brings us to what doesn't fit." Harland looked back at his notes. "Ma'am, Ms. Simms told us she brought him home. But you say he didn't arrive."

"Oh." Ellen's mind raced, searching for something neutral to say. Something that wouldn't come back to haunt her. "Did she say she actually brought him here? Or to her house? It's an easy walk from there."

Harland consulted his notes, flipping back a few pages. *"The management wanted him out of there so I brought him home.* I see your point. She might have meant just back to Penticton. Could've dropped him here, or anywhere." He snapped the notebook shut. "Alright. Well, Mrs. Hoskins, don't you worry. He'll turn up. I'll be in touch tomorrow."

Ellen closed the door behind him and leaned her head against it. Tomorrow was Tuesday. Work. What should she do about work?

She turned the deadbolt, then went to check the back door. If she showed up at work, that would look odd. Wouldn't it? Well, not really. No one but Clarissa knew that Stan was missing. And Clarissa seemed to think he was off on some wild bender.

Or did she?

What did Clarissa really think?

Something nagged at the back of Ellen's mind. She stroked Monte's silky head, rubbed his soft ears. Blinds—was that it? She filled his water dish, scooped him some kibble. "Good night, Monte." She paused in the doorway of the office, hand on the light switch.

Clarissa *had* been in here on Saturday. She had left that heavy perfume hanging in the air. Her explanation was reasonable. Wasn't it?

She said she used her own keys. Not Stan's. She didn't even seem to know that Stan's keys were in the door. Did she? Ellen had practiced her share of deceit over the last few days, and she thought she had gotten away with it. Was Clarissa playing a game of her own?

Her eye fell on the email print-out. She picked it up and carried it with her to the bedroom. Email. Clarissa knew Ellen didn't often check her email. She re-read the message, skimming past the low assessment of Stan's character and slowing down for that final line. *Get rid of that jerk.*

Had Clarissa really dropped Stan off on Main Street? She said herself Stan had never put the moves on her before. Vain as she was, wouldn't that have been something of an insult for Clarissa?

Ellen pictured it. The dim booths of the Blue Moon. Couples intimate in the corners. Quiet conversation, low music, the clink of cutlery and the occasional burst of laughter. Clarissa enters to meet... someone. Ah. There he is. A short, balding accountant with a round little pot belly and post-nasal drip. Clarissa's eyes widen in horror as he raises his hand, gestures at her, points to... a red carnation in his lapel, their prearranged sign. This guy doesn't fit the Chippendale model at all. Clarissa swears under her breath. "Liar."

Reluctantly, she crosses the room toward him. Suddenly she stops. That laugh, from the corner. It can't be.

It is. It's Stan. Stan Hoskins and some little tramp.

The accountant—Harold? Yes.—Harold stands, smiles, waits for her. His smile fades, as she stands frozen, staring at Stan. "Clarissa?" he squeaks.

No, not her real name. She would have used an alias.

Carmen? Yes. Clarissa would have liked that. Carmen. Sensuous, mysterious. Silly in Harold's nasal tones.

Harold steps toward her, and Clarissa snaps to life. She crosses to him, distracted. "I'm Harold." No, wait... he'd use an alias, too. Something bold, masculine. "I'm Hank." He holds his hand out toward her. She ignores it, continues to stare into the corner. Finally, he lets his hand drop. "Please, have a seat." Uncertain, nervous, he indicates the booth.

"Thanks." Clarissa drops into her seat, still staring into the corner. The camera fades back, taking in another booth. A lone biker sits, brooding, hunched over his pint. He, too, stares into the corner—

No, wait. He wouldn't be that obvious.

Now and then, he casts a nonchalant glance into the corner. The camera moves forward, following the direction of his attention.

There's Stan. He looks much like Harold-Hank, only not as well dressed. His hair is greasy, and he is laughing too hard, smiling too much. So is the blonde he's with. She's a scrawny little bit of a thing, all bones and bleach: bleached hair, bleached teeth. Make-up by CIL paints. Silicone boobs as big as her head. Red, red lips in her pale face; red, red nails on her fluttering hands. She laughs into Stan's face as he lights her after-dinner cigarette.

No, smoking's not allowed any more.

She laughs into his face as he pours her another glass of wine.

Swing camera back to Clarissa's booth.

Supper has been served. She picks at her food, still intent on the corner. Harold-Hank picks at his, glumly. Stan goes to the men's room. The biker signals the blonde. She scowls at him, blows a kiss his way, winks and smiles.

Clarissa watches in rapt attention as Stan returns. The blonde swallows the last of her wine and scoots around the booth to snuggle Stan. She runs her hand down between his knees, up his thigh... the table blocks the camera but it's obvious what she's doing. The biker pretends not to look. Clarissa stares.

Meanwhile, Harold pays for supper. He's ready to leave.

Now Clarissa realizes she's being dumped. Damn. She attends to Harold. Bats her eyes at him. Stretches out her long, long legs. Tilts her empty glass his way. Encouraged, he orders drinks.

Stan heads to the ATM. Clarissa's eyes follow him. The biker signals the tramp. She gives him the high sign. Clarissa sees it. Harold's leaning in for a kiss, but Clarissa ducks her head past him, watching for Stan's return.

Harold curses, throws down his napkin, leaves. Clarissa doesn't see him go. She's watching Stan shove a wad of bills into his pocket. He slides back into the booth, and the blonde's hand runs back down under the tablecloth. Stan's grinning like an idiot. The blonde laughs. Words and phrases fade in and out of the sound track: *freshen up... minute.* She heads for the washroom.

The biker drops a ten on his table, leaves. Sound of a bike firing up. Clarissa watches the door of the ladies room. The blonde scurries out. A second engine fires up. Tires squeal. Bike and car roar off.

Stan hasn't yet noticed he's been ditched. A smile curls Clarissa's lip, and she glances toward Harold.

Harold is gone. Clarissa's face creases in to confusion. Where is Harold? Men's room?

Now Stan slides around in his booth, looking toward the ladies' room. He sees Clarissa. She fakes a bright smile, then slides herself around to face the men's room.

Camera scans the room. Intimate couples, playing kissy-feely in their booths. Except Stan's booth, except Clarissa's. Time passes. Rest room doors open and close.

The light comes on for Clarissa. Now she's got to make the best of it. She stands, saunters over to Stan.

"Stood up?" she asks him, smile still curling her lip.

"Whadda ya mean?" Stan doesn't know when she got here, doesn't know how much she knows. "I just stopped in for a drink."

Clarissa is about to contradict him, but thinks the best of it, lets it go.

"Need a ride home?"

Wait. Freeze frame. Clarissa had said management wanted Stan out of there—said he was throwing his weight around—and Constable Harland said the Blue Moon backed that up. Rewind.

The light comes on for Clarissa. She frowns, bites her lip. Now the light comes on for Stan. He hasn't seen Clarissa yet. He signals to the waiter. Points to the ladies' room.

The waiter shrugs, shakes his head. He's not setting foot in there.

Stan leaps to his feet, charges across the room. Shoves the door open: empty. No. A woman screams! Not his tramp, though. Some other blonde.

Stan heads for the exit. Looks toward the parking lot. Sees—or rather, doesn't see. His date's car is gone. Waiter taps him on the shoulder. Hands him the check for dinner.

Now Stan's roaring mad. Pulls a couple of bills from his wallet. Throws them at the waiter. Waiter signals manager: phone the cops.

Clarissa stands. Holds up her hand. Action stops: the men turn, slow motion, to stare at her. Stan's face registers disbelief.

Sensuously, Clarissa crosses the room. She reaches out and adjusts Stan's tie. He gapes at her.

She winks at the waiter. "I'll take him home." Jealousy on the waiter's face, the manager's.

The cashier's a woman, though; she's not impressed. She holds up the drink check. Points to Clarissa.

Clarissa opens her wallet. One lonely twenty. She flutters her lashes. "Oh, dear. This was my gas money. What will I do?"

Stan has regained some of his composure. He's impatient. "I'll pay for the damned gas. Let's get outta here."

Clarissa drops the twenty into the waiter's hand, runs her long, red nails lightly along his cheek, blows a kiss in the direction of the manager, turns, and sticks her tongue out at the cashier as she saunters out. Manager and waiter fall to their knees as the door swings closed.

Stop tape.

Well, that was a bit much.

Oh, what the hell. It's my story.

Now Clarissa and Stan are in the parking lot. Clarissa opens the door for Stan, then swishes her hips around the front of the car. Stan doesn't even notice. He's spouting off a litany of complaints about the service, the food, the good people of Westside, and the world in general.

Clarissa starts the engine. Reaching for the gear shift, she runs one long nail up the outside of his thigh. He doesn't miss a beat.

She pulls out onto the highway. Tunes the radio station to SilkFM. Stan notices the music, adds "sissy damn radio stations" to his litany of complaints. Clarissa shuts it off. Swivels in her seat so her skirt rides up her thighs. Leans past him to open the glove box, baring ample cleavage. "Look here," she breathes. "See anything you like?"

Stan shuffles through the CDs. "Buncha sissy crap. Lookit this guy. Pink shirt. Bloody fruitcake. And that guy—" his voice goes high-pitched, singsong "—married to his fruitcake songwriter." He snorts. "Here. This is okay."

He slams a CD into the player. Clarissa finally sits up straight. She has almost driven off the road trying to hold this pose.

Razamanaz blares from the speakers. Stan bounces to the beat. He hasn't got a rhythmic bone in his body.

Clarissa winces. This CD's hardly conducive to seduction. Not a romantic song on it. They drive on, Stan bouncing. Clarissa's head is starting to pound. Holy Roller comes on. Stan jabs fast forward. "Bloody sissy Jesus-freak bullshit."

"That's what it's about," Clarissa says, irritably.

"Huh?"

"That's what they're saying. It's about people who pretend to care, people who do religion just for show."

Stan doesn't get it.

Clarissa shakes her head.

By the time they reach Summerland, Clarissa has had it. Her head is pounding, Stan is still bouncing, and she's ready to chuck Nazareth out the window. Now the car is sputtering. Damn. If she can just crest this hill.

They coast into the gas station. Stan is absorbed in the music, and when Clarissa shuts it off he starts to whine. She yanks the keys from the ignition, gets out, slams the door. Stomps to his side of the car. Holds out her hand. "Gas money," she says.

"Gas money? What gas money?"

"Okay, Stan. This is it. Pay for the damn gas or you're walking."

"Alright, alright, here's my card."

"Card? Then you go pay."

"I ain' goin' nowhere. You think I'm that stupid? I'll come out, you'll be outta here."

Clarissa straightens up. "Fine. Pay at the pump, then."

Stan sniggers, pointing at the sign. "Pay at pump unavailable," he reads, all sing-song. "Please use ATM inside."

Clarissa closes her eyes, counts to five. "What's your code?"

"Huh?"

"Your code, you idiot. I need your bloody PIN code."

Stan smiles, all crafty. "Wait a minute. How much?"

Clarissa glances at the pump. "I'll need to put in ten bucks worth, minimum."

"You go in an' get us a twenty," he says. "Ten fer the car and ten fer us. I'll make it worth yer while."

"Sure, Stan," says Clarissa. "Your code?"

"Mrs. Hosk," he says, smirking.

That takes some of the wind out of Clarissa's sails.

She stomps into the station, puts the card in the machine, punches the code. Waits. Pulls the card from the machine and stomps back out.

"What's your real code?"

Stan smirks again. "Mrs. Hosk. You know, *Ellen.* Ellen Hosk." He laughs.

She stomps back into the station. Cashier watches her try again. Watches her stomp back out to the car.

"Look, you idiot, this is the last try. Then the machine eats your card. What is your damn code?"

"Ell-en," he says. He makes the shape of an L with his finger and thumb. Traces an N in the air. "L N Hosk." He laughs and laughs.

Jerk. She stomps back to the station again. Gets the twenty. Slams it on the counter. "I'll need ten at pump six," she says. The guy behind the desk shakes his head, hands her a ten, turns on the pump. She stomps back to the car, throws Stan's card and the ten at him, pumps the gas. The attendant is still shaking his head as Clarissa peels out onto the highway.

They drive in silence to Penticton.

No, not in silence. The second the engine is running, so is Nazareth. Clarissa stops for a red light.

Her head is going to explode.

She shoves Stan out.

No, wait. Back up the tape. She couldn't just shove him out—physically impossible.

Ah. There's a cop car at the intersection. "Get out or I'll start screaming."

"Go ahead. What would I care?"

Clarissa opens her mouth and the window, screams at the top of her lungs.

No, that won't work either. Cops notice stuff like that.

Clarissa pulls the car to a stop at the intersection. Her head is pounding. She shuts off the CD.

"Whadja do that for? You got PMS er somethin'? Bloody females. I'm outta here." Stan's hand is on the door handle. The light to her left has gone amber when he opens the door, loses his balance, sprawls to the asphalt.

The light's green. Clarissa guns it through the intersection, leaving Stan swearing on the pavement.

Ellen smiled, buttoning her pajamas. So there's Stan with a whole ten bucks, loose in Penticton on Friday night. Ten dollars. Why did I—ah, ATM. Why else would Stan have insisted Clarissa use the ATM instead of just paying for the gas?

Of course, that was just the version Clarissa gave Constable Harland. She really had only Clarissa's word for it. For everything. Ellen climbed under the covers, and backed the tape up to the intersection again.

This time, Stan turns down the music. Broken Down Angel. "Jeez, I'm sorry, Clarissa," he says. "Thanks for the ride."

They move through the intersection, toward Clarissa's house. Clarissa is starting to feel lusty again, her pride's still smarting. She pulls to a stop. "You want to come in for a nightcap?"

"Hell, no. Burned out old cougar like you?" Stan climbs from the car, laughing. Staggers toward home.

For a full minute, Clarissa grips the wheel, seething. *Burned out? Cougar?* She could just *kill* Stan. She should, really. Do Ellen a big, big favor. She starts the car, rolling forward with the lights off.

Damn, she forgot about those deep ditches on Government. She'll have to be careful. Watching closely, she eases the car ahead. There's Stan. Off in the distance. Almost at York. She could just slide the car up behind him, knock him into the ditch. *Oopsie.*

What's that? A figure emerges from under the evergreens, and suddenly Stan's shadowy form drops from sight. Some teenage punk has just done the world a favor. Clarissa turns into the vacant parking lot of the grocery store, swings the car around, heads for home.

Ellen stared up at the ceiling. Had there been a car, that night? She didn't think so.

Footsteps?

Had Clarissa followed Stan?

Friday night, she had felt so powerful, so anonymous. Saturday and Sunday had been so peaceful. Today the peace was shattered, first by the thought of Clarissa's betrayal, then by the email.

Ellen closed her eyes. *i saw what u did.* Damn email. Chain letter, probably. No one else even knew Stan was missing. She knew, the police knew. Clarissa knew. Nobody else. Should she go to work tomorrow? Announce it somehow?

Work. PenWest. Her eyes flew open. Stan's boss knew he was missing. She frowned. He'd said if Stan didn't show up, he was fired. Maybe he already *was* fired.

She'd have to call there in the morning.

FOUR

MONTE WAS GROWLING low in his throat, but he hadn't yet barked. Ellen glanced at the clock on the bedside table; 2:15. She reached for her robe.

Monte continued to growl.

"What is it, boy?" She peered around the doorframe toward the darkened porch.

Monte gave a sharp bark as the area outside the porch was flooded in light. Something had activated the motion sensor.

Ellen tied her robe and moved through the dark toward the porch. Monte was standing alert, ears forward, staring at the door. Ellen reached over him and twisted the wand to open the blinds. She peered out into the darkness, listening.

A rustle, and Monte gave another warning bark. Ellen concentrated on the garbage cans that leaned against the wall of the shed. Suddenly, one of the cans tilted and fell over. Monte barked in earnest as a large gray and white cat scrambled from behind the cans and leapt onto the fence.

Ellen put her hand on Monte's head. "Just a c-a-t, Monte."

Monte didn't seem convinced. He continued to stare at the door, ears erect. "It's okay. He's gone." As she stroked his silky head, the outside light clicked off. Monte quieted and looked up at Ellen.

Then the security light came on at the neighbor's, and Monte faced the door again. "Not our yard, Monte. Not our business." Ellen smiled, reaching for the wand. Her hand froze. Monte stiffened beside her.

Something was still moving beside the garbage can. Or was it? Ellen reached for the light switch, flipped it off and then on. The back yard flooded with light once more. She peered at the garbage cans.

Nothing. Just her imagination.

The toppled can was empty; she'd leave it until the morning. She switched the light off, and started counting to twenty, waiting for the switch to reset. At the neighbor's, the outside light went out, and both yards were plunged into darkness, except for a small rectangle of light. Ellen looked up toward the house; the rectangle shone from an upstairs window. She watched a silhouette cross the window, return, and stop, framed like a shadow puppet in the middle of the upstairs wall.

Ellen involuntarily stepped back further into the porch. The shadow in the neighbor's window stared down at her, and Ellen clutched her robe tighter. Monte looked up at her. She jumped at the cold of his nose against her hand.

The shadow moved away, and Ellen sagged with relief. She flicked the outside light back on, and closed the blinds.

Keep the blinds closed.

Ellen shook herself. Really, she was being ridiculous. Absolutely juvenile. Getting all worked up about a silly prank email, imagination running wild. Oooh, a shadowy figure staring down at her... for goodness sake, she couldn't even tell whether the boy next door was looking outside or had his back to the window.

The boy. Why did she assume that the upstairs window was in the boy's bedroom? She had seen him coming and going next door, had occasionally been treated to the weary *thud-thud-thuda-thud* of heavy bass when he was home alone. More than once she had heard his mother, shrill and out-of-control, order him up to his room. *Up* to his room. Ah.

She turned on the kitchen light. The teapot and mug were still sitting out, the electric kettle had long since boiled and shut itself off. She turned it back on and opened the cupboard, trading the regular tea bag for chamomile. Closing the cupboard door, she glanced out over the kitchen sink.

The light was still on in the upstairs window. No shadows, though. She laughed. In the porch, Monte's ears perked up, and his tail thumped the floor. "Crazy, huh, Monte?" she asked, and his tail thudded faster.

Ellen poured a bit of hot water into the teapot and swished it around. She dumped it into the sink. Steam rose and fogged the window, briefly blurring the image of the neighbor's window and the figure that filled it. He was back.

The kettle whistled, and Ellen tore her eyes from the rectangle of light, forced herself not to look again. Really. What would the neighbors think, her staring up at them like this? She dropped the tea bag into the pot, poured in more boiling water, and grabbed her mug, heading to the office on the other side of the house.

She set the teapot and mug down on her desk, and turned on the lamp. Checked the blinds.

This had to stop. Ellen slumped into the armchair. Stupid, stupid email. What exactly had it said? *i saw what u did.* That was so juvenile, so silly. *Keep the blinds closed.* Well, what of it? What would anyone have seen through the blinds?

Hadn't the email called her *Mrs. Hoskins?*

She reached under the desk and switched on the power bar, then settled into the desk chair, waiting for the computer to boot up. She poured herself a mug of tea, careful not to spill.

No new mail. She clicked on the trash.

There it was.

u should always keep your blinds closed mrs hoskins. always.

It wasn't one of those ones that got randomly forwarded on to everyone in cyberspace. Unless someone was taking time to personalize. Why would anyone bother?

Just for the sake of argument, what if the boy next door had sent the email. As a prank, like kids used to do with telephones, before call display put an end to that.

What of it? It didn't mean he had seen anything, anything at all.

And what *could* he have seen? Through her windows? Generally, not much. An ordinary middle-aged woman going about her ordinary middle-aged life.

Except Friday night.

What would he have seen Friday night, or early Saturday morning?

Well, he might have seen her come in. He might have watched her put her clothing in the laundry and... oh. If she had left the light on in the porch, and the blinds open, he would have seen her strip down to her underwear and put her clothing in the washer.

Lucky him. Her underwear was as middle-aged as her body. How very unexciting.

Ellen clicked on the trash, emptied it, and shut down the computer. There was nothing anyone could have seen that would incriminate her. It wouldn't be the first time she had come in at that hour. Often, when Stan was snoring and she couldn't sleep, she had got up and taken Monte for a walk, reveling in the peaceful stillness of the night.

She frowned. Monte. She hadn't taken with her that night. Well, what of it? She could say she didn't always take Monte. Who could prove otherwise? She could say sometimes, she preferred to be all alone.

A woman? After dark?

Well, why not? Years ago, before she had Monte, she would walk for hours at night. Not since, but who could prove she didn't?

She turned off the lamp, and took the teapot and mug to the kitchen. Setting them beside the sink, she looked up at the window next door. The light was pale now, blue. Like a television was on. Or a computer screen. *Little punk,* Ellen thought defiantly. Then she softened. The kid spent most of his time in the house, alone. He probably had nothing else to do.

She switched off the kitchen light and went to bed.

THE RADIO CRACKLED TO LIFE. Ellen reached over to hit the snooze button. She turned her back on the clock and closed her eyes again, willing herself back to sleep.

It was no use. Before the alarm had come back on, she was sitting on the side of the bed, pulling on her robe.

In the porch, Monte's tail beat a slow tattoo on the floor, accelerating as she approached. She stroked his ears and under his chin, then let him into the yard. She watched as he made a beeline for the garbage cans, sniffing carefully before urinating on the one that was down. Then he followed a trail of scent to the fence, and peered into the neighbor's yard. He woofed once, low in his throat. Then he turned, head high and tail wagging, and trotted back to the house.

Ellen let him in. "Good boy. Re-staked your claim on

that garbage can?" She tossed him a treat, then went to the kitchen and plugged in the kettle.

The clock on the stove said 7:15. She sighed, then picked up the phone and dialed PenWest. She let it ring eight times, and was about to hang it up when a gruff voice came on. "PenWest."

"Oh, hello. This is Ellen Hoskins. Stan Hoskins' wife."

"Yeah?"

"Umm... can I speak to his boss, please?"

"That would be me."

"Oh. Ah... Stan is... he's missing."

"Can you speak up? It's a little hard to hear in this place."

Ellen raised her voice, and her chin. "Stan won't be in for work today. He's missing."

"Whadda ya mean, missing?"

"Well, the police are... they're looking for him."

"Looking for him?"

"Yes. He's... he's missing. He hasn't been home for days. I just thought... I just thought I should let you know."

"When'll he be back?"

Ellen pulled the phone from her ear for a moment, and stared at it. "Look. He's missing. I don't know where he is or why he's gone. I don't know when he'll be back."

"He expect us to just hold his damn job for him?"

As Ellen she searched for a reply, the line clicked dead. The guy was Stan's boss. Theoretically, that meant he was one of the bright ones at PenWest. Stan had gone to work each day with this bonehead. No wonder he'd become such a grump. Maybe she should have encouraged him to find other work, instead of...

Well. She hung up the phone, shaking her head. No point getting all sentimental over Stan now.

The clock said 7:18. Too early to phone her own boss? Probably. She'd take Monte for a quick walk first. In her bedroom, she pulled on jeans and a shirt, made the bed, then opened the blinds. The day promised to be a nice one; already the sun was chasing the dew from the lawn. Her fingers itched to get into the garden.

In the porch, she collected Monte's leash and a couple of treats. "Come on, boy." She didn't have to ask twice. Monte was through the door like a shot. He raced around the yard twice before screeching to a halt at her feet, head up, waiting for the leash. "Okay, boy. Let's go." She patted her pocket for keys, then pulled the door closed behind her.

ELLEN CLOSED THE GATE AND UNCLIPPED Monte's leash. At the neighbor's a door slammed. The dog's ears perked. He gave a quick yelp of excitement and raced through the open side gate, into the front yard.

Rounding the house, Ellen was surprised to see Monte, paws on the fence, straining toward a boy who stood on the sidewalk. The boy smiled, holding something toward the dog. Then he saw Ellen. His hand dropped, his smile turned to a frown, and he swung from the fence and slouched away.

Monte followed along the fence, whimpering, until he reached the end of the yard. He watched until the boy was out of sight, then turned and trotted slowly to Ellen.

"Who was that, Monte?" Ellen asked. Monte licked her hand. Pulling her keys from her pocket, Ellen unlocked the back door. She tossed Monte a treat. "Stay outside a while."

Was it the boy from next door? She pulled off her shoes. And what did the boy have in his hand? She glanced at the clock. Good heavens. No time for a shower this morning; she would be late for work.

Work. *Not today,* she reminded herself. It would probably be best to call in and let them know what was happening. After all, it would seem heartless of her to carry on as usual.

She dialed the direct line to her boss.

"Benders and Associates. Marge speaking."

"Hello, Marge. It's Ellen."

"Good morning, Ellen. What can I do for you?"

Ellen pulled her face into a worried frown. "I'm sorry, Marge, I can't come in to work today."

Marge laughed. "Ellen, after all these years, are you actually taking a sick day?"

"No, not really. Well, maybe I should call it... I don't know. I'm not sick. I'm..."

There was a moment of silence. Marge spoke slowly. "Ellen, what's wrong?"

"Stan's missing."

"Stan?"

"My husband." Ellen realized that no one at the office knew Stan; he'd never been available for social events.

"Missing?" Marge was all serious concern. "Oh, Ellen. Since when?"

"Friday night?"

"Friday night? Ellen, are you alright?" Marge snorted. "What a stupid question. Sorry. Of course you're not alright. And of course you can't come in to work. Are the police looking for him?"

"They are. They're trying to figure out... well, what might have happened."

"Do you need someone to come over? The company has a counselor on staff, if you want her. She's pretty good at helping people find whatever assistance they need in a crisis—"

"No, no. Thanks, Marge."

"You sure? Let me know if you change your mind. Meantime, don't you be even thinking about coming in to work. We've got a good leave policy for this sort of thing. Well, not *this* sort of thing exactly. But for a family crisis. You know."

"Oh."

"Yeah. You can have—I think it's three months at half pay, something like that. No deductions, so almost as much as you'd make coming in, so if you're finances... I mean...

I'm sorry, Ellen. I'm not real good at this. Are you sure you don't want the counselor to come over? She knows all about this stuff."

"Thanks, Marge. I don't think I'll need it." Three months without work? Ellen liked her job, and it was really the only social outlet she had. Besides Clarissa.

"Oh, no, of course you won't need it," Marge rushed to cover her latest blunder. "He'll show up. You sure you're alright?"

"Yes."

"Well, you keep me posted. Do you want me to... I mean, should I tell anyone?"

Ellen had a vision of the entire office lined up at her front door, dripping with casseroles and sympathy, asking questions she didn't want to answer, probing, searching for evidence of her distress, calculating its quality and quantity.

"Maybe not just yet," she said.

"Sure," said Marge. "We'll try to keep it quiet. I know you like your privacy. But you call if you need anything."

"I will, Marge. Thanks."

Ellen hung up. Marge was almost a friend. She felt terrible lying to her. Although, she hadn't really lied. Not really.

Three months. That would be... having the summer off. Ellen smiled. She hadn't had the summer off in... well, in years. Not since she was what, twelve? Good heavens, what would she do with herself?

Garden. She stepped into the tub and turned on the shower. Imagine a whole summer of gardening. She shook her head. There wasn't enough garden to fill up *all* her days. Long walks with Monte. Hiking! Long, serious hikes, overnight, just her and the dog. Back-packing in the mountains, sleeping under the stars. It had been years. Not since Robbie—Did she still have the stamina? Well, she could start off small.

She would *have* to start off small. How would it look to Constable Harland if she took off with the search still on? "Ta-ta, now. I'm off on a hike. See you in a few days."

She shut off the water and reached for a towel, then grabbed her robe as the phone rang. She glanced at the clock.

"Good morning, ma'am. Constable Harland here."

"Oh, good morning. Any news?"

"Nothing yet. I take it there's been nothing at your end?"

"No. He... he hasn't called, or anything."

"I'm sorry, ma'am. I'll be following up with Ms. Simms today, see where exactly she dropped Mr. Hoskins off, and we'll go from there. You alright?"

"I'm okay. Thank you."

"We have people who can help you at a time like this, give you some assistance with a variety of things. You want me to put you in touch with someone right now?"

"Oh. No, thank you."

"Alright. I'll drop off some information later on that you can use if you feel you need it. Meanwhile, don't hesitate to call."

"Thank you."

"Don't mention it, ma'am."

Really, everyone was so kind. Ellen stooped and used a corner of her robe to wipe the puddle that had formed under her feet. She went to her bedroom and closed the blinds while she dressed, then re-opened them.

Leave the blinds closed, Mrs. Hoskins.

Yeah, right. I don't think so, kid.

The sun was shining, the birds were singing, and the flower beds beckoned.

FIVE

ELLEN STIRRED THE STEW, then replaced the lid on the crock pot. She pulled the last tray of cookies from the oven and set it on the stove top to cool. As she transferred the cooled cookies from the first tray to the wire rack a blob of chocolate, still warm and gooey from the oven, stuck to her hand, and she licked it off before moving to the sink to wash.

A movement from the yard caught her attention, and she glanced up. Monte was dancing along the fence, paws up on the top rail, with his ball in his mouth. The boy from next door leaned across the fence and tossed something into the air over Monte's head. Before Ellen could see what it was, Monte had dropped his ball and snapped it up.

Now the boy was leaping over the fence. Ellen stood frozen, watching. Monte grabbed the ball, shook his head, raced in a circle, and dropped at the boy's feet, releasing the ball. The boy reached into his pocket, pulled out something and tossed it into the air. Monte leaped and snapped.

The boy stooped, patted Monte's head, and picked up the ball, tossing it toward the front yard. Monte raced off in pursuit, returning to drop the ball again. This time, when the boy reached into his pocket, he squatted. "Roll over," he said.

Ellen watched in amazement as Monty rolled. The boy tossed the treat into the air; Monte leapt, snapped, and crouched down, ready to roll again. "Dance," said the boy. Monte stood on his hind legs, placing his forepaws in the boy's outstretched hands, and the two of them turned in a circle. The boy laughed, then froze. He had seen Ellen through the kitchen window.

Ellen smiled, raising her hand to wave. But the boy had already released Monte and was slouching his way toward the back gate. Monte followed him out of Ellen's sight, then returned, running toward the fence as the boy appeared in his own back yard. He didn't look at Monte. His back door closed with a slam. Monte watched for a moment, then turned and headed for the porch.

Rock music blared from next door. Ellen glanced up at the window. Was he in his room? Perhaps playing on his computer?

Ellen went to her desk. The computer was running, and

she clicked on the mail icon. No new messages. She clicked "new mail" and typed IwatchU145@gmail.com into the address field. Subject: *Thanks for playing with Monte*. Message: *I'm sure he gets very lonely while I am at work, and I'm glad to see he has a friend to keep him company. Come visit him any time. Ellen (Mrs. Hoskins).*

She paused. What if she was wrong? What if the boy wasn't IwatchU? She shrugged. If he wasn't, what difference would it make? She re-read the message. Whoa. She was giving new information to the emailer. She deleted "Ellen," changed "Monte" to "the dog," and before she had any more second thoughts, clicked "send." As the message disappeared from her screen she exhaled, suddenly aware of holding her breath.

Ellen stared at the screen a moment, half expecting it to fill with the scowling face of the boy next door, or crude graffiti telling her where to go and how to get there. Shaking her head, she closed the keyboard drawer.

The last tray of cookies had cooled. Ellen rummaged in the back of the cupboard and found her cookie jar. She washed the dust from it and dried it carefully; it was one of her treasures, an "apartment-warming" gift from her brother, long ago, in the days when she made cookies often.

It had been years since she had baked for her own home. Stan preferred cookies from a bag, and complained when she "wasted" grocery money buying "this damned baking stuff" for home-made ones. When it was her turn to bring goodies for the office coffee break, she baked and wrapped as quickly as she could, feeling guilty, and feeling foolish for feeling guilty. It would be easier to stop by the bakery near the office, but she liked to bake, liked the smell and the feel and the taste of batter, liked the warmth she could see in the faces of the people who ate her chocolate chunk cookies, liked knowing she could mix happiness up in a bowl and serve it up to anyone.

Ellen wondered if the boy next door ever had home-baked chocolate chunks. She returned to the cupboard and pulled out an aluminum pie plate, dusted it and piled in some cookies. As she filled the cookie jar, she found herself hoping that Constable Harland would stop by, and she shook her head. *Really. You're beginning to sound like Clarissa.* Still, he seemed a nice man; courteous, kind, a bit traditional. One who would appreciate home baking.

"Don't be stupid," she said.

Monte woofed. "Coming, Monte." She washed her hands and dried them, then went to the porch.

Opening the back door, she looked down at the dog. He spun in a circle, tail wagging. "Walk time?" she asked, and he barked. Ellen reached for his leash, checked her pocket for keys, and locked the door.

THE DAY WAS GOLDEN. Children played in their yards and in the lanes; here and there someone was digging in the garden, mowing a lawn. The air smelled fresh, people smiled at each other, and the dogs they met wagged their tails and sniffed Monte courteously. No hackles, no hassles. Ellen caught herself humming *What a Wonderful World*, and as she and Monte neared home she had to restrain herself from singing out loud. The scent of lilacs greeted them even before she could see their purple and white blossoms lining her back fence.

Opening the gate, she stopped cold. Monte looked up at her, whining. The blossoms nearest the gate had been stripped from the bushes, torn away from the stems leaving long, gaping, greenish white scars. Ellen touched one of the wounds. *Probably children,* she thought. *Good thing lilacs are hardy.* Still, she wished they would ask. She would have been happy to snip them a few blossoms with her shears.

She let Monte off his leash, and he bolted to the front door for the paper, returning with it in his mouth. "Good boy," she told him. Monte dropped the paper and ran to the back door, sniffing curiously.

"What is it?" Ellen stepped around him, and her eyes

widened. There, on the back steps, were her lilacs, tied in a rough bundle with a bit of broken shoe lace. She stooped to pick them up. Under the bundle was a note scribbled on a scrap of paper. "Sorry about the message." No signature.

She turned and glanced up at the house next door, spotting a quick movement away from the bedroom window.

Ellen hung up the leash, then went to the sink, rinsed the vase, and filled it with fresh water. She untied the lilacs and arranged them, glancing up to the window now and again. She set the vase on the counter, hoping he would see them.

The computer was still on, and she checked her email. No new messages. She clicked on "new mail" and sent a quick note to IwatchU. "Thanks for the flowers." She clicked "send" and closed the keyboard drawer, then noticed the flashing light on her answering machine. Two messages.

"Ellen, Clarissa. That cute cop was here again. Can you find something else he can question me about? Please! How are you doing? No word from Stan? Call me."

"Mrs. Hoskins, this is Constable Harland. I'm sorry but we have nothing new. I'll try to contact you again later in the day." A pause, then "I hope you're alright. Good-bye for now."

Monte yelped. Ellen walked softly to the kitchen window and peeked out. The boy was leaning over the fence, rubbing Monte's ears. She grabbed the foil pan of cookies and headed for the back door. As she opened it, the boy tensed. His face worked through a scowl, an embarrassed frown, an attempt at a smile, back to the embarrassed frown. His shoulders hunched forward and he turned to flee.

"Hello," Ellen called quickly, relieved when he stopped. "Monte, introduce me to your friend."

Monte yelped, and the boy glanced back over his shoulder, then turned away again. "Glad to meet you, Aarp. I'm Ellen." She stopped a couple of feet back from the fence, rubbing Monte's head. "Care for a cookie? No, not you,

Monte. Chocolate chunks are bad for dogs. I was asking your friend Aarp."

The boy turned. He wasn't smiling, but the scowl was gone. He glanced from the cookies to Ellen, and back to the cookies. "Fresh baked." Ellen held out the tray, and Monte quivered in excitement. "Sorry, Monte. I should have brought you a treat too."

Monte yelped agreement.

The boy reached slowly into his pocket. Then, quickly, as if he was afraid he'd change his mind, he walked toward the fence. "I've got some." He tossed one into the air over Monte's head, and Monte snapped it mid-air.

"He likes those. What are they?" Ellen asked.

The boy pulled another one from his pocket, held it out.

"Looks like kibble," she said.

"It is." The boy sounded ashamed, embarrassed. "It's just the cheap stuff."

"Well, Monte certainly enjoys them. Have a cookie, Aarp."

The boy smiled. It was just a little smile, but a smile nonetheless. "Jason."

"Nice to meet you, Jason." Ellen took a cookie from the plate and bit into it. "Good thing you're around to help me eat these. I like them way too much."

Jason bit his cookie, and his eyes widened with pleasure. "Wow." He finished the cookie and reached for another one, then stopped. "May I?"

"Of course. Actually, I'd appreciate it if you took the whole pan. I've got plenty more in the house, and no one to eat them."

Jason bit another cookie. "What about your old man... I mean, Mr. Hoskins?"

"Stan doesn't like home-made cookies."

"He's crazy. Wish my mom still baked."

"How come she quit?"

Jason scowled again, and Ellen mentally kicked herself. "Never mind, that's none of my business," she said. The scowl cleared. "Thank you again for playing with Monte. He really does need lots of exercise. Come over any time."

Jason ducked his head, and Ellen could see the red creeping up his neck. "I'm... I'm sorry about that..." He looked ready to run.

"Oh, that message? We used to do stuff like that on the phone when I was a kid. No big deal." Ellen paused. "I am curious, though. How did you get my email address?"

Jason glanced up at her, then down at the ground. He scuffed his sandal along the bottom of the fence. Then he looked up at her again. "It was a dare."

"A dare?" Ellen held out the cookies, and Jason took another.

"Friend of mine dared me. We're having a... a contest." Jason ducked his head again. "It's stupid."

"What I'm wondering is, can just anyone get my email address if they want to? I thought you couldn't do that."

"Only if you leave your computer on."

"If I leave it on?"

"Yeah," he mumbled. "I mean, if you leave your computer online, hackers can get into your files pretty easily."

"But I have a firewall in my computer. I thought that was supposed to stop hackers." Ellen offered the plate again.

"It should." Jason scuffed the ground again. "Most times, it probably does, but it's still a risk."

"You must be pretty good at this computer stuff then. Planning to go into that line of work when you finish school?"

Jason tossed a kibble for Monte. "Maybe," he said. "I don't know."

"Bet there are a lot of job possibilities in that field. You have a couple of years before grad?"

"Three." Jason leaned over to pat Monte, who stood with his paws on the fence. "I don't really have any plans."

"Plenty of time," said Ellen, offering another cookie. "Oh, dear. I hope I'm not spoiling your supper."

Jason snorted. "Supper isn't til Mom gets home at ten."

"Oh. You doing the cooking?"

He shook his head. "She usually brings home leftovers from the restaurant." He poked a finger into his mouth and made a gagging noise. "I'll never eat at a fast food place again."

"You like beef stew?"

Jason sighed. "Anything but hamburgers."

"Come for supper."

Ellen was as surprised as Jason. She hadn't meant to invite anyone. Well, maybe Officer Harland. She had considered that possibility while she chopped carrots for the stew. If he came by, would she ask him to stay?

Maybe. Probably not.

Jason was looking at his feet. "Really?"

"Really. It's not much. Beef stew. Maybe cookies."

Monte stretched up on his hind legs, pushing his head against Jason's hand.

"What about Mr. Hoskins?"

Yes, thought Ellen. What about Mr. Hoskins? "Stan is away right now." She looked at Jason. "Look, I've got a big pot of stew that will be ready in about an hour. If you feel like it, come on over. Let's say about six."

"Thanks. You sure?" Jason sounded hopeful.

"I'm sure," Ellen said firmly. "You're more than welcome. Monte's already vouched for you."

Jason smiled. This was a real smile, like the one she had seen earlier when he was dancing with Monte, and it lit up his whole face.

"Thanks, Mrs. Hoskins… isn't that your phone?"

"It is. Call me Ellen. And take the rest of these cookies away with you." She headed for the door. "Bring the plate back for a refill when you come for supper."

ELLEN CLOSED THE FRONT DOOR. Constable Harland had been concerned, sympathetic. Clarissa's story had been consistent: Stan was a pain, so she took advantage of a red light and dumped him at Main Street. They were hoping to find a witness, but it would be hard without going public. How did Mrs. Hoskins feel about that?

Ellen had been flustered at the suggestion. Of course they should go public. Shouldn't they? If she said "no," wouldn't it look like she didn't really want to find Stan? Or worse, like she had something to hide?

What if she said "yes" and someone came forward? "Friday night? Yeah, I saw him walking home. Then suddenly this lady comes out from under the trees and..."

Constable Harland had interrupted her thoughts, suggesting she think about it. "I know it's hard, putting yourself in the spotlight and all, but I'm afraid it's the only way to move forward. It's too late to contact the media for tonight, but I think we should move on this tomorrow morning. Can I stop by, say nine thirty? We'll need some recent photos, stuff like that." She had smiled, faintly. Photos. Recent photos. Of Stan.

Constable Harland had patted her arm. "It will be alright, Mrs. Hoskins. I'll see you tomorrow at nine thirty."

Ellen heard the cruiser pull away and leaned her head against the door. Tomorrow, at nine thirty. Should she offer him more cookies, or a full confession?

In the back yard, Monte yelped. She looked at the clock: six. Jason was probably here. She went to the back door and opened it, the smile of welcome freezing on her face when she saw Jason heading back into his own yard, slouching toward the door. "You coming for supper?" she called.

He turned and glared at her. "You called the cops."

"What?"

"You called the cops!" Jason's neck was crimson, and he spat the words at her. "I didn't *break* in, and said I was sorry! You and your stupid cookies!" He flung the pie plate, which caught in the wind and dropped ineffectually to the ground.

"He was here about Stan."

Jason reached for his door.

"Constable Harland was here because my husband is missing."

SIX

JASON PAUSED, his hand on the knob, and Ellen crossed her yard to the fence. "Jason, it never even occurred to me to talk to the police about the email."

The boy turned and faced her.

"It was a prank, not a crime. Constable Harland is trying to find Stan. Come have supper with me."

Jason leaned on the door for a moment. Then he bent and picked up the pie plate and headed toward his gate.

"Jump the fence; I don't mind." Ellen patted Monte's head, then turned toward the house. "Bring your appetite. There's plenty."

Jason put one hand on the top of the fence and swung himself over. "You in track?" Ellen asked. "Hurdles, high jump?"

"Nope." Jason's head was still down, but the color was going out of his neck.

Ellen opened the door, and the aroma of beef stew and cookies wafted out. Jason stepped in behind her and stood on the mat while he removed his sandals. Monte padded across the porch and selected one of his favorite toys. He dropped it at Jason's feet. The boy leaned down toward the dog. "This your toy?" He rubbed Monte's ears, and Monte eyed his sandals. "Are my shoes in your way?"

"He'll lie on your shoes, if you let him," warned Ellen. "It's a compliment. He'll only do it if he likes you. And don't worry—he won't chew them."

Jason looked at Monte. "Sure, you can lie on my shoes. Keep them warm for me. Bet you won't lie on the old man's..." He stopped, and the color crept back up his neck.

"No, you're quite right," Ellen hastened to reassure him. "I'm afraid Stan and Monte didn't get on well. Monte was a starving little stray who wandered into our yard one day, while I was in the garden. He spent the afternoon with me, and when Stan got home he said we'd best get rid of him. I did try to find his owners; no luck." She cut three slices of bread and set them on a plate. "If Stan had his way, the pound would have had poor Monte."

In fact, Monte *had* gone to the pound. She had come home from work on a Monday afternoon to find him gone, and when she'd asked Stan who had come for him, the sarcasm of Stan's reply had tipped her off. "Some real dog lovers," he'd smirked. Back then, they still had the car; she had driven across town to the pound, returning with Monte and a lighter wallet. Stan had sworn at her, raised his hand and then eyed the bandage on her forehead. He'd stomped out of the house and not returned until the wee hours, stinking of stale beer and cigarettes.

Monte had tried to stay out of Stan's way. The following Monday, when she had arrived home from work, Stan was gone. It was not unusual for him to go to Jugs for lunch and make a day of it. She'd found Monte quivering under the back steps, and when she finally coaxed him out, she cried. There was a gash on his nose, and a mark on his paw that she suspected was a cigarette burn. The next morning, she was at the table when Stan stumbled into the kitchen. She stood, pulled herself to her full height, and faced him. "You will not hurt Monte again." It may have been the only time in their marriage she had stood up to Stan. She took Monte for a walk, and later that day she applied for a shift change. From then on, like Stan, she'd work Tuesdays through Saturdays.

Jason was giving Monte a belly-rub. What had he seen, in the rare times that Monte and Stan were home alone?

She didn't want to know.

"Supper's ready, Jason."

"I should wash. Can I use your bathroom?"

"Sure." Ellen realized that Jason already knew where her bathroom was, and had a moment of doubt. Had he been watching her? Really watching, and not just casually glancing out his window and, from time to time, noticing the couple next door?

"Have a seat." She dished stew into the bowls. Jason sat in the chair nearest the porch. Monte thumped his tail against the floor.

Ellen opened the fridge. "Milk? Juice? I'm afraid I don't have any pop."

"Milk, thanks. Pop is right up there with burgers."

Ellen laughed. "A teen who's sick of pop *and* burgers. Who'd have thought such a thing was possible?" She passed him a glass of milk and set the carton on the table. Jason waited politely until she sat down, then picked up his spoon.

"This smells great." He took a bite. "Mmm." He closed his eyes.

"I'm glad you like it."

Jason looked across the table at her, his face sober. He swallowed. "How come…" He stopped.

"How come what?"

"How come you're being nice to me when I…"

"Who hasn't done something dumb in the past week?" She buttered a slice of bread, and pushed the other two slices toward him. "Have some bread. No hamburger buns."

Jason smiled again, the bright smile that lit up his face. He took a slice and buttered it. Then he laid it on his plate.

"Look, Mrs. Hoskins…"

"Ellen."

"Ellen… you might want me to leave, but I have to tell you, I was… I came into your house."

Ellen forced herself to continue chewing. She swallowed. "Oh?" She took a sip of milk. "When?"

"A couple days ago. I didn't break in or anything. I was… I was playing with Monte and I saw the keys… in the front door. It was that stupid dare." The color had risen again in Jason's neck. He looked miserable.

"So you came in and got my email address?"

He nodded. "You had a printed one on your desk."

"Well, I'm glad to hear you didn't hack into my computer." Ellen took another sip of milk. "What else did you do while you were in here?"

"Nothing." Jason rubbed his foot against the floor. "I know you have no reason to believe me, but... I just got the email address and left."

"Did you happen to close the blinds?"

Jason stared at her, blankly. "Blinds?"

She waited.

"Oh, blinds. That 'you should keep them closed' crap. No." Jason looked puzzled.

Ellen blew on her stew. "What was this dare all about?"

Jason fiddled with his spoon. "Me and a fr... My friend and I, we were having an argument. He said you could change somebody's behavior if you made them uncomfortable. We were watching one of those stupid movies where somebody gets a phone call and they suddenly are so creeped out they start living their life totally different."

Jason took a bite of his stew and chewed, swallowed. "I said it would take more than a phone call. He said it wouldn't. He said one creepy call would be enough. I said, no way. He said he'd prove it. I said, how? He said, he'd call somebody and tell them he was watching them. I said, yeah, but how about call display, and star-six-nine, and all that? And he said email, then." Jason swallowed a mouthful of milk. "He said he could just email somebody an anon... anona..."

"Anonymous," said Ellen.

"Yeah, an anonymous message, and that would be it." Jason tore off a piece of bread and dunked it into his stew. "I said no way. He'd just make up stuff to prove he was right. He said fine, I could try it myself. I said it wouldn't work. He said it would, and he'd bet me he could get somebody to change their behavior before I could." Jason put the bread in his mouth, chewed and swallowed. "Said we'd have to pick somebody with a routine. I said, my neighbor, she does everything routine. Like clockwork. Before I knew it, I'm on the wrong side of the argument. I mean, before I was saying it couldn't be done. Now I'm betting I can do it faster than him. And I've got my stereo on it."

"Your stereo?"

"Yeah." Jason tore off another piece of bread. "He bet his skateboard. I bet my stereo." He made a gun with his fingers, pointed it to his temple. "Stupid."

"Oh, dear." Ellen got up from the table. "Excuse me, please." She went to the living room, the bedroom, then the office. When she got to the porch, Monte watched as she closed the blinds.

"Sorry I have no blinds in the kitchen." Ellen sat, picked up her spoon. "How long do I have to keep them closed?"

Jason grinned. "Two days should do it."

"Do they have to stay closed all day?"

Jason considered. "That might get kinda hard to take. How about from supper time on?"

"Done. More stew? Or dessert?"

"That was great, Mrs. Hoskins…"

"Ellen."

"Ellen. Can I have just a little more?"

Ellen half-filled his bowl. Setting it in front of him, she said with mock severity: "Okay. So, the blinds will stay closed in the evening for the next two days, but only on one condition."

Jason froze, spoon halfway to his mouth. "Condition?"

"You may *not* keep that boy's skateboard."

Jason smiled with relief. "No, ma'am. And no more dares. At least not ones that involve other people." He ate a bite of stew. "How come you and Mr. Hoskins never had kids?"

Kids? There'd been a time when she yearned to have

children. By the time Monte came along, she was aware she never would. And she was glad. She fingered the scar under her curl.

"I'm sorry." Jason looked uncomfortable.

"Don't be. It's a normal question. It just never happened." She smiled. "So you're not in track?"

"Nope. I tried out, but I'm not good enough."

"Not fast enough this year?"

"Not fast enough, not strong enough. You know. Not good enough."

"Any other sports?"

"Nope." Jason wiped his bowl clean with the last of the bread. "I *hate* team sports."

"Maybe next year. Things change pretty fast at your age. From the little I've seen of you since you and your mom moved in, I'd say you've grown a lot the last few months. My brother was all arms and legs at your age, no coordination. The next year, he was a little more used to his body's new shape and size. He got on the spare list for a couple of track events in the fall, and in the spring he got to participate in a couple of meets the usual athletes couldn't attend."

"He win anything?"

"Not that year, but the points for participation helped his team. Next year he came home with a few ribbons."

"After that?"

Ellen set her spoon down. "Robbie died in a car accident that year."

Jason swallowed. "I'm sorry."

"It was a long time ago."

"Must have been awful for your family."

"Robbie was my family. We had lost our parents when we were really young, and got shipped from foster home to foster home. We were lucky, though: we always managed to stay together, until the last move. I was luckier than Robbie; I was with nice people. He wasn't. Robbie was two years younger than me. As soon as I finished school, I got an apartment and Robbie came to live with me. We each worked a couple of jobs in the summer, and when school started again he kept working. He was catching a ride to work with a friend after school. I always wondered, if I'd left him in that home…"

She closed her eyes. The unexplainable accident, car hurtling down the bank to the railway tracks, Robbie dead at the scene, the young driver in a coma for weeks… This was more than Jason needed to hear. "I'm sorry, Jason. This isn't something I usually talk about."

Jason ran his finger around the rim of his empty glass. "My dad died in a car accident, too. Last year." His voice lowered to a whisper. "It was my fault."

"What happened?"

"He was coming to pick me up after soccer practice."

Ellen became aware of the clock ticking. In the porch, Monte whimpered in his sleep. The evening sun cast shadows through the leaves of the trees, reflecting crimson and gold dapples of light that spilled in through the window and onto the tablecloth.

I hate team sports.

"How would that have made it your fault?"

Jason scowled. "I thought *you* would understand."

"Understand?"

"Yeah. You said if you'd left Robbie at the foster home, he'd still be alive. He wouldn't have been going to work."

"Oh." Ellen's eyes widened. "I suppose he could just as easily have been on his way somewhere else."

"Yeah, but he wasn't. And my dad died because I played stupid soccer. And now my mom has to work at a job she hates, and she never cooks or bakes any more, and that's because Dad died, so that's my fault too."

"I should have left Robbie in the foster home."

"Why? You said they weren't nice people. I bet you made him cookies and bread and beef stew, and I bet you were happy. I bet Robbie was happy. How do you know it wouldn't have happened anyway?"

Ellen nodded. "You're absolutely right."

Jason's stared at her. His face suddenly softened. "I get so mad at people when they say it wasn't my fault, and here I'm…"

"I guess we can't very well take responsibility for things we have no control over. But you know, all these years, I did feel responsible."

"But you shouldn't have."

"No," Ellen agreed. "Should you?"

Jason picked up his empty glass, turned it around in his hands a few times, slowly. Finally, he set it into his bowl. "Maybe not."

Ellen smiled. "Cookies?"

"I'm kind of full. That stew was so good, Mrs. Hosk… Ellen." Jason stood and took his dishes to the sink. "Want me to wash these?"

Ellen looked at him in surprise. "Thanks, Jason. I'll get them organized." The crock pot was still half-full. "Would you like to take home some stew?"

"Really? Maybe Mom'll eat it." Jason turned from the sink. "Hey, can you show me how to cook it?"

"Sure." She handed him the dish soap.

"Only thing is, I'm not sure we can afford it."

"Well, vegetables are cheaper than meat." Ellen spooned the stew into a couple of containers. "If you get a soup bone from the store, and boil it for broth, it usually has a bit of meat on it. Then you just add more veggies, and barley. Barley is good and it's filling." She used one of the bowls to fill the empty crock pot with warm, soapy water.

"We have one of those," he said, nodding at the crock pot. "You don't put them in water, do you?"

"No, and it gets kind of baked on. You can leave it to soak." She dried the dishes, noting that Jason had already rinsed out the sink and hung the dishcloth neatly over the tap. "Thanks for your help, Jason."

"Thanks for the supper. Guess I'd better hit the books. I'll see if I can get a soup bone on the weekend." Jason headed to the porch and sat down beside Monte, reaching under him for his sandals. "Can Monte have the bone when we're done with it?"

"I don't usually give him bones. He eventually crunches them up into slivers. Besides, what if he decides to bury them? There go all my flowers!" Ellen waited until Jason stood up, and passed him a sour cream container full of stew, two slices of bread, and the aluminum pie plate, refilled with cookies.

"Thanks, Mrs. Hos... Ellen." Jason paused with his hand on the doorknob. "By the way, I'm sorry to hear about Mr. Hoskins. How long has he been missing?"

"Since Friday night."

Jason whistled. "You think he's gone for good?"

Ellen blinked.

Jason colored. "I'm sorry. That sounded... stupid. I mean... he's your husband."

"It's okay, Jason. Stan wasn't a very friendly man."

"Anyways, if you miss him, I hope he turns up soon."

Ellen smiled. "Thanks, Jason. Say hello to your mom for me. I'd like to meet her too."

"Yeah." Jason paused on the step. "My mom, she hasn't always been... I just wish you could have met her before."

"I'm sure things will get better, Jason." Ellen rubbed Monte's head. "Things always get better in the spring."

SEVEN

MONTE BARKED, and there was a quick knock at the back door. Ellen put the crock pot upside-down in the drain rack and dried her hands as the door swung open.

Clarissa stuck her head in. "You still speaking to me?" She patted Monte, who glanced at her discarded sandals, then went to his bed. He never slept on Clarissa's shoes, even though he liked her. Ellen suspected it had something to do with the cigarettes.

"Of course I'm still speaking to you. Sorry I didn't call you back. I had company for supper."

"Oooh! You go, girlfriend. Harland said he was on his way here."

Ellen snorted. "Clarissa, you have a one track mind." She filled the kettle and plugged it in.

Clarissa shrugged. "He's not married. I asked him. On your behalf, of course. With Stan out of the way, you need to get on with your life." She dropped into a chair.

Ellen turned and looked at her in surprise.

"Oh, Ellen, how stupid of me." She slapped her forehead. "Look, I just meant... okay. I *do* kind of hope he's gone for good." She bit her lip, wrinkled her nose. "Sorry."

Ellen reached for the tea pot. "Clarissa, it's kind of hard to get on with my life, as you so neatly put it, when I don't even know what happened to him."

"Fine, fine. Good, actually. That leaves Constable Harland for me."

Ellen smiled. "Blueberry or straight?"

"Blueberry, if there's any Amaretto left." Clarissa grinned as Ellen pulled out a small bottle of Amaretto, and another of Grand Marnier. "Girlfriend, you can't tell me you ain't celebrating."

Ellen rolled her eyes.

"Cookie jar! You've been baking." Clarissa leapt to her feet and strode across the kitchen. "Chocolate chunk! You *have* been holding out on me." She plunked the jar in the middle of the table. "Dish, Ellen. All the dirt. How was supper with Harland?"

"It wasn't Harland."

"Okay, then who? Tell me it was a guy."

"Well." Ellen put two mugs on the table. "Where do I begin? He's very nice mannered."

"He," Clarissa repeated around a mouthful of cookie. "Excellent. Nice mannered?"

"Yes." Ellen poured water into the tea pot.

"And?"

"And he has a terrific smile."

"Nice manners, terrific smile, yeah, yeah, and?"

"Monte likes him."

"Monte is very discerning. He didn't like Stan."

Ellen frowned.

"Sorry. Go on."

"Hmm. He's young."

"Young? A*wright*. You go, girl."

Ellen rolled her eyes again. She would never get used to middle aged women talking like college girls.

"Nice car?" Clarissa dumped Amaretto into each mug.

"No car."

Clarissa frowned. "No car?"

"He's too young."

Clarissa stared at Ellen. *"How* young?" she asked sternly.

Ellen laughed. "Look. I didn't say I had a *date*. I said I had company for supper. *You* decided it was something else." She wiped a drip from the rim of the bottle, and licked her finger. "The boy next door, Jason, is on his own at supper time. His mom works. I invited him for supper."

"Oh." Clarissa managed to look relieved and disappointed at the same time. She sipped her tea. "So. Back to Harland. What did *he* have to say?"

"Nothing new." Ellen looked at her cup. "Except he wants to go public."

Clarissa groaned. "Damn, Ellen. That's the last thing you need."

Ellen raised her eyebrows.

"I say let sleeping dogs lie. No offence, Monte." Clarissa set her mug down. "If Stan wants to be gone, let him be gone. No skin off your nose, right? Unless, of course, you want him back."

"You think he just took off?"

"I don't know why he would. You're a pretty good meal ticket, and not very demanding. He had it made in the shade with you." Clarissa reached for another cookie. "Damn, these are so good. You should open a bake shop. Anyways, if he didn't take off on purpose, then some kind soul took pity on the rest of the world and offed him. Good riddance, bad rubbish."

"You really think that might have happened?"

"Maybe. Who cares? Look, El, the man was… is, sorry… is your husband. But he's a *jerk*. Nobody likes him. He kicks dogs, he spends all his money on booze and other women, he leaches off you, he's offensive—I don't know why they let him into Jugs; even in *there* he pisses everyone off, and I'll bet they'd kick him out except he spends so much money. He scared the Girl Guides last year when they were around selling cookies, for god's sake. I've seen him scream at your neighbors, at the cashiers at the grocery store, at the lady that drives the ice cream truck, and at the kids who wanted to buy ice cream. I don't know why the hell you married him, or why you stayed with him, except you're too goddamned nice to tell him where to get off. Even that day when he had you by the hair, whacking your face into the counter, damn him, and you should have right then just filed for divorce. You had a *witness,* for godsakes. And six stitches to the forehead. And for what? If you stayed married for the vows—well, they're vows *he* didn't care about. There's no kids, thank god, and no other family to miss him. I'm not sure anybody actually gave birth to him and if they did—well, his mother probably kicked him out young for beating up his baby sister. The man was a *monster,* Ellen. Good riddance."

Ellen looked up from her tea.

Clarissa fidgeted in her chair, drummed her nails on the table. "Damn. Ellen, I'm sorry. I just think… If Stan *is* gone… well, take care of yourself for a change. And hell, if some nice guy comes along and wants to take care of you, let him."

I'll take care of you now. Ellen closed her eyes. Stan, at her elbow as they lowered Robbie's coffin into the ground,

"Don't worry, Ellie girl, I'll take care of you now." The fog of grief, the cloud of apathy, the waves of inertia that ever so slowly ebbed away until she awakened one morning to realize just what her emotional absence in that first crucial year of marriage had wrought.

Who knew what their marriage could have been, would have been? She remembered little of the few dates she'd had with Stan before Robbie's accident; snippets of conversation, mostly. A cameo of Stan under the hood of his car, whacking at the engine with the wrench and swearing, then climbing behind the wheel and smiling smugly when it roared to life: "Works every time. Gotta know how to take care of things." But she couldn't remember how she really felt about Stan before they married. All of her memories had been colored by her growing awareness of Stan's cruel temper, each one's brightness and contrast distorted by the passage of time.

"Really, El," Clarissa persisted. "If that Constable Harland offers to take care of you, why not?"

Ellen opened her eyes. "That's how I ended up with Stan."

Clarissa was silent for a moment. "Well, damn, girl, I'm not saying marry him or move in with him. I'm saying let him take you to supper. Let him take you out dancing, for godsakes. You used to love to dance. I betcha he knows how. These chivalrous types always do."

Ellen smiled. "What would this chivalrous-type guy think of me out dancing, and my husband's body hardly cold?"

"Aha! You think Stan's dead."

Damn. "Okay, okay. It does make the most sense." Ellen steadied herself, took a breath. "I find it hard to imagine anything else. Maybe he's run off with another woman—"

Clarissa snorted.

"Precisely," Ellen continued. "It's not likely he's been kidnapped and held for ransom. He was always making up stories, pretending to be more important than he was.

Maybe he said the wrong thing to the wrong person, made them think he knew something he didn't."

"You mean, like, drug dealers, big time theft?" Clarissa took another cookie, sat back in her chair, munched thoughtfully for a minute. "Okay, I see it now. Stan's on his bar stool at Jugs, overhears the guy next to him talking about a car that's been stolen, or a bike. Let's make it a Harley Fat Boy, brand new, owner only had it two days. Stan's little ears start to tingle, his beady eyes light up. Here's an opportunity to be important. He leans over, 'Hey, mister, you oughta check that back yard on Government and York. Watch out for the wacko who lives there, though. There's a bike or two gettin' pulled apart behind that fence.' He smiles, expecting the guy to buy him a beer, welcome him into the inner circle, offer him a seat at their table."

"But he hasn't looked behind him—"

"And there, standing behind him at the bar, is the friendly neighborhood gangster from the local chop shop—"

"Who waits for him outside the bar—"

"Yeah, 'cause he knows Stan'll be walking home."

"So he waits."

"Calls his buds to get the yard cleaned up, just in case the guys inside don't know Stan and actually *listened* to him—"

"Yeah, and then he waits for Stan to come out," Ellen agreed.

"Then, he follows Stan, waits for his moment, clobbers him—"

"Stan's route would have taken him past the chop shop."

"Yeah, good. Clobbers him right there and drags his body into the garage." Clarissa bit another cookie. "No! How about this! Government was all dug up! How about he clobbers Stan and dumps him into the ditch, breaking his sorry neck! The trucks come the next morning, cover him up. Voila! Stan the snitch is history!"

Ellen's mouth had gone dry. Her hand shook as she poured herself another cup of tea.

Clarissa was caught up in her story. "No, that won't work. They would have seen him there in the morning, and you'd've heard about it by now. But you have to admit it would have been the perfect crime. Cops would've thought he was staggering home, drunk, and fell in the ditch."

"Yeah, except they can usually establish that the clobber came before the neck broke, and if he wasn't killed by the fall you'd have some explaining to do if you climbed into the ditch and finished him off." Oh, god, time to shut up.

Clarissa shook her head. "But if that's where they found him, dead after getting drunk and stumbling into a ditch, why would the cops waste their resources looking further?"

Ellen reached for a cookie. "You'd think they'd always do a thorough examination."

"Only if the cause of death isn't obvious or doesn't make sense."

"You sure about that?"

Clarissa shrugged. "Pretty sure. I kinda looked into it when I was considering getting rid of Dave."

Ellen's eyes widened. "Clarissa, you weren't serious!"

"I probably wasn't. I was furious, absolutely fed up, and I really did think life would be so much easier if I just didn't ever have to deal with him again."

"Tell me you're not still thinking that way."

Clarissa laughed. "Past tense, girl. I said I *thought* about it. But those prison uniforms? Not my style. Besides, things really aren't as bad now, or at least I'm getting better at coping with his crap." She bit another cookie, talked around it. "I think... I think the trick is to have a plan ready for when he screws things up." She swallowed. "Because he will. Take this thing with him and that Martha clone. It's got him acting like a father, even though it's for the wrong reasons. I should celebrate, but I'm really not that nice a person. I know it won't last. So, I can wait for it to collapse, have him not show to collect the kids when I have to be at work in an hour, and then I can wring my hands and whine, 'Oh, poor me, he did it again.' Or, I can have the lady next door on retainer, so if—no, *when* it does happen, I'm ready. I don't even have to think about it anymore."

Ellen frowned. "On retainer?"

"Yeah. She doesn't go out much in the evening, and it's not really any problem for her to be available for my afternoon shifts. If she's got something she wants to do, and all of a sudden I need her for my little angels, she'll drop it and come."

"Why on earth would she agree to that?"

"Simple." Clarissa was fidgeting. "I take her to bingo each morning on my way to work when I'm on day shift. And she generally catches a ride when I'm on evenings, too."

"How does she get home?"

"I pick her up on my way home. Except when I'm on evenings a friend brings her home. Hall closes before I get off."

"She plays bingo *all day?*"

"All day, every day." Clarissa grinned. "Says she actually makes money at it. I'm not sure that's possible but who am I to argue? Played bingo once in my life. Dead boring. Haven't set foot in one of those places since." She stood. "Look, Ellen, I gotta have a smoke. Wanna walk me home, you and Monte?"

"Sure. Hey, Clarissa, I need some recent photos of Stan. Constable Harland wants them for tomorrow morning. I haven't taken any pictures in years, but your boys took some at the birthday party you had for me last month, remember?"

"Yeah. I'm not sure Stan's in any of them though. Didn't he flip out and leave before we even cut the cake?"

"Can we have a look?"

"Memory card's still in the camera, so sure, as long as the boys haven't taken it to their father's." Monte's tail thumped as Clarissa reached for his leash. "Come on, girl. Leave the mugs on the table. I need my smoke!"

ELLEN UNLOCKED THE BACK DOOR, calling Monte to come in with her. She picked up his empty dish, washed it and filled it with fresh water, and returned it to the porch. Scooping kibble from the bag, she thought about Jason and how well he and Monte got along. The boy needed a buddy, someone who would simply accept him, the way Monte did, and not dare him into trouble. She shook her head. That was just kid stuff. His friend was probably just as harmless, acting with the thoughtlessness of youth, not intending to be cruel.

Before Friday night, would that silly email have bothered her in the least? After all, she had just buried her husband in a ditch. What was it they called that on the news… the correct term for improperly disposing of human remains? Offering an indignity, or something really weird-sounding like that. A crime, anyway. So of course the kids' prank made her jumpy.

Ellen put the plug in the bathtub and turned on the tap. She went to the bedroom and reached to close the blinds. They were already closed. The blinds. They were the only thing she still didn't understand. Of course, with Clarissa's perfume in the office, Jason's message on the email, and Stan's body in the ditch, maybe she was making too much of blinds being closed. She was ordinarily a creature of habit, "like clockwork" as Jason had pointed out. But her usual habits didn't include late night burials and early morning wallet disposals. Maybe, that morning, she had simply forgotten to open the blinds. Or, even more likely, she forgot to open the blinds now and then, and in the ordinariness of every other day, simply didn't notice. Maybe the only reason she attached any importance to the fact they were closed was because so many other things that day were out of sync.

Monte munched contentedly in the porch. Ellen went to the bathroom, checked the water and adjusted the taps. She stripped, dropping her clothes into the hamper. In the porch, the back door rattled as Monte, settling on the mat, leaned against it. Ellen climbed into the tub and sank into the soothing warmth. She felt safe. Calm. Clarissa's wild theory about the chop shop had gotten a little too close to the bone, but that was just Clarissa. All talk, all the time.

Ellen sank deeper into the water, reached up with her foot and turned off the tap. It was quiet in the house; no wind outside, no rain. Peaceful. No need to brace herself against Stan's noisy return from Jugs.

Jugs. Clarissa went in there on occasion, but Ellen couldn't fathom why. The once she'd ventured in had been enough. Of course, Clarissa had more spunk than Ellen ever would. Raucous men didn't bother her, and she could drink with the best of them. A naked woman prancing on stage wouldn't have made Clarissa blush and look away; after she and Dave split up, she'd gone regularly with a friend or two. Ellen suspected she really did it just to show how tough she was. Stan had seen her there once, complained about that damn friend of hers, can't keep her mouth shut, showing up at *his* bar, wrecking *his* evening.

His complaint sounded likely: Clarissa'd sized the peeler up, estimated the cost of her boob job, critiqued her choice of music and her ability to entertain, and then provided a running play-by-play, just like when she and Ellen watched figure skating. "If the girl wants to dance bebop, why the hell did she pick a reggae song? And what's with the bloody cowgirl outfit? Somebody should teach her some rhythm."

Stan had told Clarissa to shut up: damn female, what would she know about stripping? Think she could do better?

Damn rights, she'd said. Next amateur night, be there.

Bad bluff. At least, Ellen hoped it was a bluff. Stan never missed amateur night. First Friday of every month.

Ellen frowned. First Friday.

Clarissa and Stan, sitting alone in their booths at the

Blue Moon. He stands and saunters over to her. "What the hell're you doin' here? Aren't ya s'posta be makin' yer debut at Jugs?"

"In your dreams, Stan."

"Yeah, yeah. I always said you was all talk, no action."

Clarissa slams down money for the drinks. They squabble all the way to Summerland. By the time they hit Penticton—

No, Clarissa would probably have killed Stan herself by then, cooped up in the car all that way, him taunting her like that. More likely—wait, wait. The first of the month *was* on a Friday. Amateur night was the week before.

Quit borrowing trouble, Ellen scolded. She wondered briefly if Clarissa had gone ahead with it. Not likely. Surely she wouldn't go that far. Odd that Stan hadn't commented one way or the other: "that slut friend of yours" if Clarissa did get up on stage; "that chicken-shit friend of yours" if she didn't.

Maybe Stan had been out with a woman on amateur night, too. Maybe he didn't even know whether or not Clarissa had shown up to bare all.

Clarissa liked to have a good time, but surely stripping was too much, even for her. Why did she bother with places like Jugs? Ellen kicked herself mentally. Man hunting, of course. But why Jugs?

Ellen kicked herself again. More men than women, there. Men quite willing to buy a drink for someone like Clarissa, men quite willing to ogle her, shore up her confidence. Especially after the internet date not working out.

Of course, Clarissa's date might not have been that bad. Nasal-tone Harold, the pudgy, balding accountant, was just a character in Ellen's own script. Besides, even her Harold might have been dashingly romantic; bald was often sexy, the pudge might have disguised a flare for dance, the nasal twang might have been only a temporary symptom of first-date jitters.

Ellen mentally clipped Harold from the booth at the

Blue Moon, set him on the bar stool at Jugs. The door swings wide and Clarissa stands in the opening, silhouetted against the night. The glance of every male in the place swivels her way, then freezes. Clarissa holds the pose for a moment, then saunters toward Harold. "There you are, big boy." She cups his chin in her hand. "I've been looking for you."

Every other male in the place groans, looks down into his beer. Harold's jitters go into overdrive. His voice squeaks so high it breaks glasses behind the bar. "Carmen. How did you find me?"

"Babe magnet like you? Simple." Clarissa has hold of Harold's neck tie. She lifts him from his bar stool, pulls him toward a table like a dog on a leash. He follows gratefully.

She circles a table, sinks into a chair while leaning across the table top to pull him into his. "Down, boy." She raises her hand to the bar. "Two over here." She looks across at Harold. Frowns when she realizes he's staring past her, not at her. Glances over her shoulder.

The door has opened, and Stan is heading for his usual stool. "Shit."

Harold watches Stan, and Clarissa waves her hand in front of his face, tugs his neck tie. "Hey, bub. Ignore that jerk. You're here with *me.*"

That's stupid, thought Ellen. Clarissa's internet date lives in Kelowna. At least, that's what she said he'd told her. Anyway, he wouldn't be at Jugs.

Ellen erased Harold and replaced him with a sleazy-looking blonde in her early twenties. Clarissa regards her curiously. "How come you do this, girl? Pay any good?"

No. Clarissa came to have her ego stoked.

Ellen erased the blonde and penciled in a businessman in a rumpled suit. Still not right. She replaced him with a bearded, tattooed biker.

Stan leans in from his stool. "You say yer missin' yer precious Fat Boy? You otta check that chop shop at York and Government."

Ellen's eyes flew open. God. What if Clarissa hadn't been making it up?

Of course she was. The bartender said Stan hadn't been there that night.

EIGHT

THE BEDSIDE CLOCK said 5:14. Ellen pulled herself upright. It was no good. Sleeplessness had finally given way to tortured dreams: Stan clawing his way through dirt and asphalt, then scaling the fence at York and Government, only to have his head crushed by a crow bar, a sinister woman in a trench coat looking on, Clarissa's throaty laugh and heavy floral perfume wafting like smoke from under the evergreens. Constable Harland tapping his notebook, dark glasses reflecting her white face and ill-fitting prison dress: "But your prints were on the murder weapon, Mrs. Hoskins. What have you done with the body?"

She pulled on her robe, went to her office and turned on the computer. A few games of solitaire might put her to sleep. In the porch, Monte thumped his tail against the floor. Ellen went to him and patted his head while she waited for the computer to boot up. "It's too early, boy. We'll go out in a bit."

Returning to the office, she played a couple of rounds of solitaire, quitting when she realized her mind wasn't on the game. She clicked on her email. One new message. She looked at the address: jason9000. Subject line: thanks for supper. She clicked the message: mom says thanks for the stew and the cookies she wants the resipee! can she have it? her next 1-job day is friday. come for coffee if u want in the morning l8r jason ps this is my real email address.

Ellen replied: Of course she can have the recipe. I'll write it out for her tomorrow. Come by & visit Monte & pick it up after school. Ellen.

She sent the message, then went to the kitchen and filled the kettle. She wondered what Jason's family had been like before his dad died, whether his mom stayed home more, cooked "real" meals, baked cookies. Ellen rarely saw the woman; once she been waiting at the bus stop outside the neighborhood grocery store, wearing a restaurant uniform, visor in hand. What was it that Jason had said, "her next one-job day"? She was working two jobs, then, to support them. What a shame. There must not have been any life insurance. Or not enough.

They must have done okay while his dad was alive; Jason had his own stereo and his own computer. Although he may have gotten a used one, or his parents' cast-off. Ellen had gotten hers dirt cheap when the office upgraded, paying for it over five months with deductions from her check. She hadn't found it terribly useful, but it was handy for banking. Of course, that meant being connected to the internet, which cost money too.

The internet. Jason had said that some hackers could get into her computer; probably true. She returned to the office and shut the computer down. Monte was sound asleep again, whimpering softly. Ellen made herself a pot of tea and a slice of toast. The cookie jar was still on the table.

Pulling out her recipe box, she found the spattered card filled with childish scrawl. *Aunt Millie's Chocolate Chunk Cookies.* She had long since lost touch with Aunt Millie— some distant relative who pinched cheeks, knitted socks and made wonderful cookies. Aunt Millie was apparently not in a position to take in children when Ellen and Robbie found themselves orphaned; nor were the few other relatives whose shadowy figures populated Ellen's dim recollections of early childhood.

In one of Ellen's clearest memories from the time she and Robbie referred to as B.C.—before crash—she was "helping" her mother spoon dough onto cookie sheets, while Robbie sat on the floor licking a beater. Her father breezed in from work, kissed his wife on the top of her head, hugged Ellen, accepting the lump of dough she popped into his mouth, and managed to side-step Robbie's gooey hands before sweeping the giggling toddler up into the air.

When the people came to pack her parents' things, they didn't bother with her mother's recipe box. For some reason it had been tossed into a carton with Robbie's toys. Ellen had seized it, and each time she and Robbie changed foster homes it was the first thing she packed. When they were in the rougher homes, the ones she came to see as endurance tests, she lived in fear of losing that box; in these places, family members believed the children were not entitled to any privacy and went through their things whenever they wished, taking whatever they wanted, keeping whatever they liked. Before long, Robbie's few toys had been ruined by other children.

When they were in their third such home, Ellen began to keep the recipe box in her school back-pack, which she guarded carefully. Leaving it at school was too risky; once they had changed homes suddenly, moving across town overnight and starting at another new school in the morning. They were not given the opportunity to return to their old school to say good-bye to classmates and collect their things.

Most foster homes were not so bad. Some truly welcomed Ellen and Robbie, treating them almost like family. One of the nicer mothers enjoyed baking, so Ellen had asked one day if they could make chocolate chunks. Chocolate chunks? Mrs. McConnell had a chocolate chip recipe. Was it the same? Ellen shook her head, ran to her room, and came back with the card. The cookies were an instant hit, and Ellen and Mrs. McConnell spent many happy hours in the kitchen.

When the McConnells were transferred to Cache Creek, Ellen realized too late that the recipe had gone with Mrs. McConnell's box. She had pulled a blank card from the back of her mother's box and written the recipe out from memory, tears streaming down her face at her loss.

Loss of her mother's recipe card? Loss of the McConnells? She didn't really know. Perhaps it went all the way back to the loss of her parents.

Bewildered, Robbie had joined in her sobbing, and the two of them sat on the dingy gray bedspread of their new endurance-test home, holding each other and crying until Robbie had asked what was wrong.

What was *wrong?* Didn't he *know?*

Of course not. This was just the way life was for Robbie. He didn't even know it *should* hurt until he saw his sister's pain.

That was the last time he would see her cry.

Robbie. How different life could have been. Could have, should have, would have. If her parents hadn't gone on the business trip together. If their plane had stayed on the runway until the storm had blown over. If Aunt Millie had taken them in. If the McConnells hadn't transferred. If she had left Robbie in the foster home. If.

It held awfully big power for such a little word.

In the porch, Monte stretched, rattling the door in its frame as he pushed his back against it. She really should get some new weather-stripping this fall. No rush. Monte stretched, stood wagging his tail against the door, thump-rattle thump-rattle thump-rattle. Ellen smiled. Maybe it wouldn't hurt to get the weather-stripping right away.

"I'll just get dressed, Monte." She put away the recipe box, leaving the new card on the table. She stopped at the bathroom for a quick shower, dressed, made the bed, and opened the blinds. Monte had settled onto his mat again, and he rose hopefully. Ellen looked at him. Jason was right when he said she had a routine. Monte liked regularity too; change seemed to put him on an uneasy alert. She picked up his leash. "We'll be making some new routines, boy. Time we had a few adventures."

THEY TOOK A LONG, meandering walk, heading uphill to explore the streets at the top of Duncan Avenue, then back down to wander the lanes beyond Government Street.

As Ellen opened the back gate, Monte raised his head and barked. Ellen opened the side gate and he raced into the front yard.

He returned accompanying Constable Harland around the corner of the house, watching him closely. "Hello," said Constable Harland. "I'm a bit early, I'm afraid." He leaned toward Monte, holding out his hand. Monte kept his distance.

"No problem," answered Ellen, smiling.

Monte relaxed, sniffed the outstretched hand, then allowed the man to pat his head. Ellen unlocked the door, and Monte pushed past her into the porch, emerging with a ball between his jaws. He dropped it in front of Constable Harland's shiny black shoes.

Ellen regarded the dog with surprise. "Monte has just given you his seal of approval."

Harland laughed. "I'm honored," he said, tossing the ball toward the front yard.

"You should be. He usually isn't that quick to decide." She held the door open, watching as Monte returned, dropping the ball again at Constable Harland's feet.

"That's enough, Monte. Come in, please, Constable. I don't think I have any recent photos of Stan. Clarissa thought she might have some on the camera, but her kids had it at their dad's. If you'll excuse me, I'll start up my computer and see if she found any."

"Certainly."

"Can I offer you a coffee?" Ellen asked from the office. "Some tea?"

He shook his head. "No, thanks. Glass of water would be nice though. It's going to be a scorcher."

Ellen poured a glass of water for each of them from the filter-pitcher in the fridge and put a half dozen cookies on a plate. She passed one of the glasses to Constable Harland

and carried the other and the plate of cookies into the office. "Might as well come join me," she said. "Could you please bring a chair?"

Clarissa had sent an email with a link to a photo site.

Constable Harland leaned forward to look at the photos. The first one had Monte sitting, Ellen kneeling on the lawn with an arm around him. He'd turned and given her a slurp up the side of her face just as Clarissa snapped the picture. Ellen's nose was wrinkled, her smile wide, her eyes creased with laughter.

Three shots of Clarissa's boys, Ryan and Justin; one of her cat, Doofus, snoozing on the couch in a patch of sunshine. Then Ellen's birthday party.

Ellen opening gifts, Justin "helping" rip the paper. Ellen dishing up cake, Ellen cutting the cake, Ellen blowing out candles. A wildly crooked shot of Ellen sitting at the picnic table, lemonade in hand, watching smoke and flame erupt from the barbecue as Clarissa turned the hamburger patties. Ryan, secret agent 009-and-a-half, had the camera and was racing about "shooting" people, hollering "gotcha" each time he took a picture.

Of course, Stan had not been amused. He probably would have grabbed the camera and stomped on it if he wasn't so afraid of Clarissa.

Afraid? Odd choice of words. Ellen realized with surprise that Stan *was* afraid of Clarissa. Even before that day in the kitchen, when Clarissa had yanked open the back door, stormed into the kitchen, picked up a butcher knife with one hand and the phone with the other and told him he could either let Ellen's face up off the counter or find out if 9-1-1 could get to him before she did.

"Nice photo."

Ellen glanced up. Constable Harland was pointing to the picture of her and Monte. She smiled. "Monte's great at slobbery kisses."

He reached for his water, and Ellen pushed the plate toward him. "Help yourself."

She returned to the photos, clicking to the next page of the gallery. And there was Stan, leaning from the lounger, glaring into the camera, clenched fist coming up from the hip. The photo was blurry, as though the camera had jumped. The next one was Stan too, this time unaware that he was being captured on camera, beer in hand, sneering toward Clarissa.

"They look good," said Constable Harland.

Good? She looked at him, puzzled.

He reached for a cookie. "You make them yourself?"

"Oh. Yes. Family recipe."

"That reminds me, Mrs. Hoskins. Have you contacted Mr. Hoskins' family?"

Ellen shook her head. "There really isn't any. His mother left him this house when she died; I never met her. No brothers or sisters. I don't think he knew his father." She pointed to the two photos, smiling apologetically. "This is Stan."

He leaned forward and looked at the photos. He bit into his cookie. Chewed thoughtfully, still staring at the photos. Then his eyes widened, closed. Opened. He swallowed again. "These are wonderful."

Ellen smiled. "Thanks."

Constable Harland finished the cookie, swallowed some water, then leaned toward the computer screen. He studied the photos for a moment.

"These the best you have?" He reddened. "I mean, are they a good likeness?"

Ellen nodded. "I'm afraid so."

Constable Harland looked up at her. "I'm sorry. I mean… he wasn't particularly photogenic, then?"

"He didn't like to have his picture taken. Clarissa's little boy didn't know that."

"A little boy took these?"

"Ryan. He's nine and a half."

She finished looking through the photos. Justin, sticking out his tongue; Justin licking icing off his finger; Justin sticking his finger into the cake. "Sorry, that seems to be it for Stan," she said.

"Oh." He studied the photos again, reaching absent-mindedly for another cookie. His third, Ellen realized. She smiled.

He looked up. "Well. I guess this is the best of the two. That one's kind of blurry."

Ellen turned on the printer, loaded it with photo paper. "How many?"

"Just one. We can copy what we need." He pointed at the screen. "What's this, a neck brace?"

Ellen nodded. "He'd been in an accident."

"I'm sorry. Was he hurt bad?"

"Not really. The taxi that he was in hit a car coming onto the parkway. Stan got a couple of bruises, complained of whiplash." Another get-rich-quick scheme. The taxi company had given him a settlement; she had hoped to put it against the mortgage but it was all spent at Jugs. "I'm sorry there's nothing else. Unless they have something at work?" Ellen suggested. "Maybe an employee I.D. card or something."

"That's a thought. I'll swing by the factory on my way back to the office." He flipped open his notebook, consulted his notes. "PenWest. Foreman didn't have much to say on the phone." He tapped the page thoughtfully. "You know anything about his employee benefits there?"

Ellen shook her head. "Stan was pretty secretive with his paperwork." He liked to shred it into tiny scraps and dispose of some of them in the garbage can outside, some in the kitchen trash. Early in the marriage she had learned never to open his mail; the telephone and electricity had both been disconnected in that first year, reconnected in Ellen's name only when she agreed to accept responsibility for staggering amounts past due.

Stan filed his own income tax, and Ellen had never seen a paystub.

She sighed. Constable Harland must think her a fool.

He was standing. "Thanks for the cookies, ma'am. I'm afraid I made quite a pig of myself." He grinned sheepishly at the empty plate.

Ellen reached into a desk drawer for a manila envelope. "I'm glad you enjoyed them. Do you need anything else?"

He returned his chair to the kitchen. "I think that's all for now."

"Will there be much…" Ellen swallowed. "Will there be much publicity?"

"Well, it's hard to say. Depends on what kind of day the media is having. Right now we just have a missing person, and we still don't know if Mr. Hoskins just went on a little unscheduled vacation. There's no reason to suspect foul play, or anything like that. The media can be very helpful with this sort of thing." He smiled reassuringly. "If we're stuck with using this photo, we'll crop it so it's just Stan. And I think we'll hold off on the media until I've asked around a bit more. Anyplace else Stan went besides work?"

Ellen slid the printout into the envelope. "Jugs. Stan was a regular there. Monte, that's enough." The dog was pushing his head into the police officer's hand, demanding a rub.

"That's alright. Good boy, Monte. You take good care of your lady, okay?" Constable Harland smiled down at the dog, stroking his head. Ellen passed him the envelope. "Thanks. I'll let you know what I find out. And thanks again for the cookies."

"You're welcome." She closed the door. "New buddy, Monte. Maybe we'll fix him up with Clarissa, so you can see more of him." She returned to the computer, smiling at the picture of Justin sticking his tongue out at his brother.

Constable Harland would be good for the boys, good for Clarissa.

Ellen felt a quick pang of—what on earth was that, jealousy? "Don't be stupid," she said, shutting off the monitor.

ACT II

NINE

CONSTABLE HARLAND PULLED INTO the vast parking lot at PenWest, following the signs that pointed to visitor and office staff parking. He eased the cruiser between a couple of rusting pick-up trucks, one with a dirt bike strapped into the back, the other sporting a platform for carrying snowmobiles.

Walking toward the entrance, he noted that in this lot trucks outnumbered cars by a huge majority; his was one of only four. The beat-up sedan and the muscle car fit in, but he wondered who owned the sporty little Honda. Maybe a visitor, but he'd bet office staff.

He was right. The Honda beeped as a tall blonde woman wearing a blazer and jeans emerged from the building, pointing her remote. She reached up to remove her name tag, then stopped, smiling at Harland. "Can I help you?"

"You might be able to, Ms. Wilkins," nodded Harland,

glancing at her name tag. He held out the photo of Stan. "I'm trying to locate this man. Stan Hoskins."

Ms. Wilkins had leaned forward to look at the photo, and drew back. "Stan. Well, I know Jack is ready to kill him. He hasn't shown up for work all week. Actually missed a shift last week, too; Saturday."

"Does he often miss work?"

"He's often late, but usually drags himself in. Jack—that's Jack Allen, his foreman—hates it when the guys come in late. Stomps into the office he shares with me to call home and yell at them. Lucky me." She grinned. "I've been Jack's admin support for a couple of years now, and he had to call Stan pretty regularly. Stan must be awfully good at what he does. Anybody else just gets canned."

"Canned?"

"Yeah. Three lates in a month and you're sent packing." Ms. Wilkins folded her arms. "But from what I hear, Stan's been a problem from day one."

"Is there anyone here that he hangs around with? A buddy, anyone like that?"

"Not that I know of." She shook her head. "I met his wife once. Was surprised how nice she was. How's she doing?"

Good question, thought Harland. There was steel in that soft little body. This morning over cookies, he'd found himself—

Ms. Wilkins put her hand up to her mouth. "Oh. I shouldn't have asked that. It's just I haven't heard from her. There are family benefits she should be aware of… stress counselors, stuff like that." Ms. Wilkins fished in the bag that was slung over her shoulder. "Could you give her my card? My hours are on it. I'm only here mornings. If she calls before eleven this number will ring straight to my line, so she won't have to talk to Jack. He's kind of a jerk sometimes, and he'll probably be mean to Mrs. Hoskins just because she had the poor sense to marry Stan." She smiled. "Just between you and me."

"Of course." Harland took the card.

"Good luck with finding her husband." Ms. Wilkins opened the door of her Honda, then turned. "Have you tried asking around at Jugs?"

"That his hang-out?"

"Yeah. He had a thing for talking about the dancers. Real perv. Liked to go on and on in great disgusting detail, see if he could embarrass anybody in the lunch room. He tried it in my office a couple of times but I kicked him out." Ms. Wilkins settled into her seat. "Give Mrs. Hoskins my sympathies. Be a blessing for her if he never turns up again. Just between you and me." She waved, closed her door, and started the engine.

Harland tucked the card into his notebook. So far not one person really cared that Stan Hoskins was gone. Except maybe his boss.

The receptionist ushered him through the office, down a long hallway, up a flight of stairs and through a heavy door. The noise inside the factory was almost unbearable. She pointed across the shop floor to Jack Allen, waving to get his attention before she turned and left.

The foreman scowled, raised one finger toward Harland, mouthed the words "just a minute," said a few words to one of the workers, then walked across the floor. "In my office," he yelled as he approached. Harland followed him, grateful when the door closed, cutting down the sound.

"You find Hoskins yet?" Jack Allen pulled his earmuffs down to his collar and settled his burly frame into the desk chair, waving Harland into the chair across from him.

"I'm afraid not." Harland flipped to a fresh page in his notebook. "I'm trying to get some more information, maybe a few leads. Is there anyone here that Mr. Hoskins was friends with?"

Allen shook his head. "Best try down at his watering hole. Jugs."

Harland looked up from his notebook. "Are you the manager here, Mr. Allen?"

"Foreman. Manager's off on one of his working vacations in Vegas, Reno, someplace."

"Is there anything you can tell me about Mr. Hoskins?"

"Lousy worker. Bad attitude, always late for work, lots of customer complaints." Allen shook his head.

"Doesn't sound like a stellar employee."

"I'd'a fired him years ago, but Barry put the kibosh on that."

"Barry's the manager?"

"Yeah, Peter Barry. No idea why he kept Hoskins on. Seemed he liked him about as much as the rest of us. Plenty of opportunities to fire him but kept him on anyway. Musta had something on—" Allen ran a hand over his forehead. "Jesus. You go to Barry with that, I'll be fired."

Harland looked over his notes. "You say that although Hoskins was not a satisfactory worker, you kept him on at Mr. Barry's request."

Allen sighed. "Thanks. Hoskins has been a thorn in my side for years. I don't mind saying I hope he's blown town and never comes back. I'd just like to know one way or the other. We've gotten real busy and I need to re-hire soon." He shook his head. "Course, I guess I can hire somebody temporary-like. Just in case." He looked up as one of the workers knocked on the glass. "Yeah, Brad?"

The young man poked his head in the door. "Sorry, Jack. We need you out here." Harland realized the shop had grown quiet.

"Problem?"

"Nothing too big, we hope."

The foreman looked at his watch. "It's almost eleven thirty. Tell the guys they can knock off for lunch a couple minutes early, and if they don't have plans they can come back a couple minutes before twelve and we'll get things rollin'. Problem solvin' on an empty stomach ain't productive." Brad nodded and left.

Harland stood. "Can I talk to the people who worked with Mr. Hoskins?"

Allen shrugged. "Sure." He stood and pulled open the door. "Brad!"

The young man turned back.

"Cop here is looking for Hoskins. Introduce him to the crew, and tell the guys to co-operate."

"Sure thing." Brad led Harland over to where a cluster of men grouped around a machine.

"Gotta be this hose, here," one of them was saying. "Blame it on Brad. He ain't around to defend himself." They turned, laughing good-naturedly, but silence fell as they saw Harland.

Brad grinned. "Guys, this here's the cop that's lookin' for Stan. Jack says to help him out."

"We'd appreciate it if you wouldn't find him," said one of the men, and the rest of them grinned in agreement.

Harland noted the name on the man's coveralls. "Jim?" The man nodded. "You worked with Mr. Hoskins long?"

"Been here fifteen years; Stan's been here almost as long."

"You know anything about his friends, interests, where he goes after work?"

"Jugs. That's about it." The rest of the crew nodded. "Oh, and he's got a wife."

"Nothing else?" Everyone looked blankly at each other.

Harland tried another tack. "He eat lunch here?"

Jim rolled his eyes. "Yeah. That's why nobody else does. We all got sick of listenin' to him. If he ain't comin' back, we'll be celebratin'. Look, maybe you could do us all a favor and just let sleeping dogs lie. We're a production crew, everybody gotta pull their weight, and that man weren't no use to nobody. 'Cept maybe his wife, but she's prob'ly better off with him gone and a bit of insurance money in her pocket."

"If she's lucky," a stocky, bearded man chimed in. "He was always makin' a big deal 'bout how no wife'a his was gonna benefit from his death. Said he was leavin' it all to his girlfriend."

Jim shook his head. "Hell, Butch. That was just Stan yappin'. There weren't no girlfriend."

Butch shrugged. "If you say so."

"He ever mention this girlfriend's name?"

"Different one each week," said Butch.

"Each day," argued Jim.

"Latest was Lucile. Lulu. Something like that." Butch frowned. "Wasn't he going on about some kinda hot date he'd lined up for Friday night?"

Jim rolled his eyes.

"Loucette. That was it. Loucette." Butch shrugged. "That was last week's, anyways."

Harland looked at his watch. Eleven thirty-two. "I'm sorry, I've cut into your lunch break."

Jim nodded. "We're kinda hung up on a problem here."

"Jack says go for lunch and we'll solve it after we've eaten," Brad put in.

A horn sounded in the parking lot. Jim turned to Brad. "Gut wagon's here. Run and tell 'er we'll be out for some of 'er fine food. Butch, go see if Jack wants anything. We gotta get this machine up and runnin' if we want the order out today."

Harland pulled out a handful of cards and passed them around. "If you think of anything else, let me know."

He didn't expect to hear anything.

A WAVE OF STALE BEER STINK WASHED over Harland, and he blinked to adjust to the dim interior. Every eye in the place turned his way, most scowling slightly before turning away with feigned indifference. The bartender placed both hands on the bar, palms down, and leaned forward, flexing his beefy forearms. "What'll it be?"

Harland pulled out the photo. "Seen this guy in here?"

The bartender glanced at the photo. "Stan? He's a regular."

"Been here lately?"

"Not on my shifts. I been off a coupla days. Hey, George. You seen Stan lately?"

A scrawny old man in a rumpled three-piece suit and tennis shoes swiveled on his stool, looking in the direction of the bartender. "Stan ain' been in here fer awhile."

Harland turned to George. "Can you remember the last time you saw him?"

George ran a hand through his long gray hair, flashed a toothless grin. "Been right peaceful here since... oh, mebbe las' Wensdey?" He peered down into his beer. "Can' recall."

A door behind the bartender opened, and a middle-aged man in jeans and a Jugs t-shirt approached the bar and picked up a microphone. He glanced at Harland, then at the clock. He turned on the mike. "All the way from downtown Burnaby, let's give a Jugs welcome to the luscious, the lovely, Lucinda." He waited a second until a skinny woman with impossibly huge breasts and impossibly blonde hair stepped through the side curtains of the stage. Flicking the mike off, he punched a button on the stereo, and music started to throb. He leaned toward the bartender. Under the lackluster applause of the patrons, he asked "What's up, Carl?"

Carl shrugged. "Cop's lookin' for Stan."

He looked at Harland. "Tim Keeler, manager. You're looking for Stan?"

"He's been reported missing. Hasn't been home since Friday morning. Anyone here seen him since then?"

"Friday." Keeler's brow furrowed. "Yeah, he was in here Friday night, late."

Carl shook his head. "I don't think so. His wife called on my last shift, Saturday. He hadn't been in the night before."

"You sure it was Friday?"

"Sure I'm sure." Carl poured another beer and slid it toward George, who was drumming on the counter. "Stan's *always* here Friday nights, but that night he wasn't.

And his wife called the next day, looking for him. That was a first."

Keeler's brow was furrowed. "I could have sworn he was here, close to closing time. Wasn't that the night Cami quit?"

"Yeah."

"And I figured she'd be back to raise hell. I sent you down the far end to bus tables and I covered the bar so I could keep her quiet. Remember?"

"That's right. She'd dumped a tray full of damned glasses in the aisle in front of the cans. Big bloody mess." Carl scowled. "Took me damn near to closing to get it cleaned up."

"That's when Stan came in. He was pissed off 'cause his usual stool was already in use. Sat over there," Keeler pointed to a table for two, near the corner.

"Was he with someone?" Harland asked.

George cackled. "Stan, wiff someone?" He slapped his knee gleefully. Carl gave him a look, and he quieted, but his shoulders still shook with laughter.

Keeler ignored George. "Nope. Least, he came in alone. He usually sits down there." He indicated the stools lining the stage.

George leaned over and whispered conspiratorially, "Gyno row."

Keeler continued to ignore George. "Stan chats up the dancers. Most of the regular girls know he's good for a drink or two, and one of them usually joins him after their show." Keeler was watching a young man in a Canadiens cap, who was leaning from one of the stools and reaching toward the dancer. She stood bent at the waist, gazing at him from between her knees as she slowly unhooked a garter and peeled off a stocking. Keeler raised a hand toward a burly man who stood near the back door of the bar, talking with a patron. The bouncer's head snapped toward the stage, and he and Keeler watched as the stripper blew a kiss at the hockey fan, who settled back into his seat. The dancer mouthed "good boy," dangled the stocking across his cheek, ran it along his shoulder and draped it over his cap. The bouncer sauntered closer to the stage.

Keeler looked back at the cop.

"Did any of the dancers join Stan that night?"

"Stan got in late, like I said. Dancers were already being looked after."

George started to cackle again. "Stan was jus' shid oudda luck that night. Shid oudda luck."

Harland turned to him. "Did you speak to Stan that night?"

George's cackle turned up a notch. "Speak to Stan? His royal majesty, Mr. Wall Stree' hisself? Guy thinks he's Donald fockin' Trump. Low-life like me gets all uppiddy and above myself, akchully *talk* to him—boy, tha'd piss him off."

"So, you didn't speak to him?"

"I *aluz* speak ta him." George corrected, his cackle so loud that even the heads in gyno row swung his way and the dancer paused mid-act to flash him an angry look. "Jes' love ta piss him off." He chortled and took a gulp of beer.

"Did you speak to him *that* night?" Harland asked again.

George had started to cough, spraying beer. Carl shoved a couple of napkins at him. "George never makes it past six o'clock here."

Keeler nodded. "If anybody talked to Stan, it wasn't George."

George, who had not yet finished coughing, slid from his stool, pulled out a cigarette and stuffed it in his mouth while shuffling to the door. When he reached the entrance he lit the cigarette and inhaled deeply, setting off another fit of coughs as the door swung shut behind him.

Harland turned to Keeler. "You remember who else was in here that night?"

The music was winding down. Keeler glanced toward the stage. The stripper, now completely naked, was writhing in front of the Canadiens fan. Keeler reached for the microphone. "The usual. Bikers, businessmen, businessmen with bikes." He flicked on the mike. "Let's hear it for Lucinda! Up next, we'll have another young lady who loves to strut her stuff. Don't go away, folks, Miss Demeanor be here to show you her ticket book in just ten minutes." He put the microphone down, pushed a button on the CD player. "Hey Carl."

Carl turned from chatting with the bouncer.

"You remember who else was in here Friday night?"

Carl shrugged. The bouncer narrowed his eyes. "You cops find any of those bikes yet?"

Harland nodded. "Just two, the Suzuki and the Gold Wing."

"I don't give a shit about those two." The bouncer flexed his chest. "I mean the Harleys."

Keeler looked back at Harland. "That's who was in here Friday night. Helmet and Jenkins. Crying the blues about their stolen bikes. They were sittin' over there, near where Stan sat."

Harland made a note. "You happen to know Helmut's last name?"

George was shuffling back to his seat, the butt of a half-smoked cigarette stuffed into the greasy hair behind his ear. He laughed, patting the top of his head. "Helmet ain' his real name."

Keeler rolled his eyes, rapped on the bar. "You guys know their names?"

Carl and the bouncer shrugged indifferently.

"Sorry, man." Keeler smiled insincerely, then his eyes lit up slightly. "Guys were talkin' with that real dishy broad. Long red hair, legs that don't quit. What's her name?"

"Whatever you wan' it to be," George cackled.

"Candy," said Keeler. "Candice, Clareese, some damn thing. Knows Stan. She was in here talkin' to the guys when Stan came in, and they had some words. She lit outta here. You best talk to her."

Harland kept writing.

Keeler looked at the men. "You guys know her name?"

They shrugged again. Keeler said "shit" under his breath.

"Stan follow her out?" Harland asked.

"Nope. He left just. Before closing time. As usual. Alone." Keeler said it with finality.

Harland pocketed his note pad. "Thanks for your time."

"Don't mention it," said Keeler.

As Harland headed for the door, George crowed "Y'all come back now, y'hear?" Blinded by the sudden daylight, Harland was grateful when the door banged shut behind him.

He walked toward his cruiser, then changed his mind and doubled back, ducking into the coffee shop on the corner. Settling at one of the metal tables, he flipped through his notes, searching for his two interviews with Ms. Clarissa Simms.

TEN

"HEY JOHN. SARGE WANTS to talk to you." Angie perched on the edge of Harland's desk, the leather of her holster creaking against the wood.

"Thanks. You know what about?"

She shook her head. "Not sure. He's been doing paperwork all morning, prepping for the press conference about that budget fiasco later this afternoon. Wants to talk to you before they get here. Might have something to do with your missing person. You getting anywhere with that?"

Harland sighed, shook his head. "Angie, you've been here forever, so you've seen it all." He raised his hand to ward off the blow she was sending his way. She laughed, opened her fist and dropped her hand to her own head, raking her fingers through her short gray curls.

"I'm simply deferring to your infinite wisdom, your vast experience, your uncommon common sense," Harland soothed.

Angie straightened her back and tilted her head regally. At fifty, she was the most experienced cop Harland knew. But the main reason he bounced things off her was because she regularly told him to trust his own instincts if he thought she was on the wrong track.

"So," she said. "What've you got?"

"Not much." Harland fished the photo from his notebook. "This is the missing Mr. Hoskins." He grinned at Angie's low whistle. "Yeah, charming. So far, nobody's sorry he's missing. Fact is, they'd rather we stop looking."

Angie's eyebrows arched. "Even his wife?"

Harland looked down at his notepad. "He drank away his paycheck, scared small children and cheated on her."

Angie's eyebrows dropped immediately. "Well then. Good riddance to bad rubbish."

"Exactly." Harland agreed.

"You think he's dead?"

Harland shrugged. "The guy didn't have any money to run off with. Unless he was blackmailing somebody. Which is a possibility. Couple of people where he works hinted that the management had kept him on when they would have fired anybody else. The man had no assets, no credit cards even. Certainly no reason I can see that anyone would kidnap him, hold him hostage."

"Medical conditions?"

"None. Although the wife didn't know everything about him." Harland looked glumly at his notebook again. "I don't think she knew about his cheating, until I told her."

Angie's eyes narrowed. "What's she like?"

"The wife?" Harland smiled again. "Nice lady. Little thing." Someone you wanted to take care of. Take on long walks. Take home to Mom.

Angie tilted her head. "I see."

Harland shook himself. "She seems pretty confused by

the whole situation, not sure what to do." He tapped the photo. "Doesn't really want the publicity."

"Something to hide?"

Harland's head shot up. "I didn't mean that. I mean, she likes her privacy."

"And she *didn't* like dear old… what's his name?"

"Stan. Stan Hoskins."

"Well, lots of women don't like their husbands. Doesn't really mean a thing," said Angie. "Especially since nobody else liked him, either. Where was he last seen?"

"Jugs, near as I can figure, at closing time. He left alone, on foot. Just spoke with the staff there."

"Lucky you. Does George still live there?"

Harland nodded.

Angie grinned. "Last person Stan spoke to?"

"Couple of bikers. They were in the company of a woman, from the description most likely Ms. Clarissa Simms, friend of the wife's. Stan was with her earlier in the evening, over at the Blue Moon in Westside."

"The plot sickens."

"Not necessarily. They were there with other people. Sounds like he got ditched and she gave him a ride back to town. Dumped him on Main. He ended up at Jugs."

"So you've spoken to her?"

"Couple of times." Harland flipped through his notes. "She didn't mention having seen him at Jugs later that night, but then, I didn't ask."

"You think she was covering up?"

"Not really. First time I interviewed her, she didn't know he was missing. Second time, I specifically asked where she had dropped him off." He shrugged. "She just answered what I asked."

"Not a talkaholic, then," said Angie. "You're going to ask her?"

"I will." Harland tapped the notebook, frowning. "The bikers she was with, Helmet and Jenkins. They owned two of the bikes that have been reported stolen."

"This guy was talking to them the same night he disappeared?"

"Yeah. You think there might be a connection there?"

"Might be. Just as easily might not." Angie frowned. "Helmet and Jenkins. That would be one Arthur Jenkins and his trusty sidekick, Mr. Andrew Flett. Also known as Helmet, because he avoids wearing approved headgear."

"You know these two?"

"They're my file. Stolen bikes case. Come over to my desk, laddie, and let's see what we can find." She paused. "On second thought, let's stop by the sergeant's office. Bring that charming portrait with you." Harland reached slowly for the photo, and Angie patted his arm maternally. "Don't you worry, now. The sergeant believes there's enough violence on TV. He won't want that mug on the evening news, scaring all the good citizens of the South Okanagan. Besides, with your latest info I'll want him to hold off until we can find out if Stan's disappearance is in any way linked to these bikes."

HARLAND LEANED BACK IN HIS CHAIR, stretching his arms down behind him. Angie's stack of files hadn't contained much of interest: six bikes stolen in three weeks. The Gold Wing had been recovered with an empty gas tank two days later in Kelowna, behind a mall dumpster, undamaged other than the ignition, which had been jimmied with a screwdriver. The Suzuki sport bike hadn't fared so well; its original colors had been coated with enamel spray paint, and it had been ridden hard before being abandoned under a freeway overpass near Kamloops. Both bikes were stolen during the night, from their owners' driveways. Harland noted the addresses: same street, three blocks apart.

He reached for his coffee. It had long since grown cold, and he stood and headed for the lunch room. Angie greeted him, coffee pot in hand. "Need a warmer?"

"Please, but I think I'd better start from scratch." He

dumped the dregs in the sink. "What's your take on these motorcycles?"

"Well, I've got a pretty good idea what's going on." Angie filled his mug and poured cream into hers. "But first I'd like to hear what you think."

Harland settled into the chair across from her. "Well, the Gold Wing and the Suzuki were probably taken by a joy-rider. Both were wheeled away from their respective homes, then hot-wired with a screwdriver. I'm thinking they were both taken by the same person; the crotch rocket first, for a trip to Kamloops and area. It was missing for what, two weeks? So somebody was having a good time. Report says the engine is seized, so now the guy is without wheels. Then the Gold Wing vanishes, the day before the Suzuki turns up. Not much fun after the sport bike, so the guy doesn't bother to alter the paint. Just ditches it after he empties the tank. I'd say keep an eye on the sport bikes in the surrounding area; if it is the same guy, he'll be itching to ride again soon."

Angie nodded. "Pretty much what I had figured. Except I'm open to the thief being female." She grinned. "Equal opportunity."

Harland nodded. "Of course. At any rate, I'll bet he-slash-she lives in the neighborhood, and knows what's available."

Angie nodded again. "I've done a couple of evening drive-bys. There were two more bikes on the street both times, one in the nine-hundred block and one in the eleven-hundred. Plus two in the eight-hundred area, and four more within a couple of blocks of there." She sipped her coffee. "And that's just what I could see. Probably more tucked away safely in garages, sheds."

"So he-slash-she has a variety to choose from."

"Drop the he-slash-she. It probably is a guy. So there are a lot of bikes in the area, but only two are newish sport bikes. A BMW decker, three more Harleys, two more Gold Wings."

"Grandad bikes?"

Angie smiled. "One of the Harleys is a pretty little chopper. But it lives with a couple of serious-looking Rottweilers. Safe storage at its best. The others are deckers, tour bikes; unless our thief knows his scoots, he'll assume they'll handle like the Gold Wing."

"Meaning?"

"Well, Gold Wings are built for comfort on long trips, and they're not known for being particularly manageable at high speed in corners."

"Okay. So they're tour bikes. And so are the others— deckers, you called them?"

Angie nodded. "Yeah. Comfortable on long trips, but they can corner decently at high speed. Not really what they're made for either, but in my experience Harleys and BMWs tend to handle a bit better than Gold Wings. In the right hands."

"So unless the thief knows how to ride, they'll leave the tour bikes alone."

"And except the chopper and the two sport bikes, the others really are clunkers."

Harland rubbed his temples. "A clunker is...what?"

She grinned. "That's not a bike term. Lots of fun, but not really prestigious enough for the discerning thief."

Harland shrugged. "Depends on whether they want to be seen, or just want a good fast ride. Take *your* bike. Most people think it's just a quiet little unassuming rice-burner. I've heard rumors of guys on big, expensive cycles dissolving in tears after you've blown past them."

Angie grinned. "Hush now. I don't blow past anyone."

"Not that anyone could prove it was you. Just a little blue blur, whipping by on the highway."

"John Harland, you know I always ride within the legal speed limit."

"Right," agreed Harland solemnly. "Anyway, unless our thief knows a lot about bikes, she will probably stick to ones that *look* fast."

"Ah, now she's a she?"

Harland shrugged. "And I don't think the four Harley thefts are related to the other two."

"No?"

"No. Each was stolen on a weekday, during working hours. Two are from the east side of town, one from Uplands and one from West Bench. None have turned up."

"Notice anything else?"

"Yellow vans, seen in the area three of the four times." Harland flipped open his notebook. "The neighbor across the street at West Bench saw a plumber in a yellow van, so did the next-door neighbor at Uplands. One of the east side locations had a carpet cleaner in their driveway for twenty minutes, seen by two of the neighbors. Nobody remembers the name of the plumber, or the carpet cleaner. The other place, no one in the neighborhood saw anything."

"So we pretty much have the M.O."

"Right. Plus there's a pattern in the thefts."

Angie's eyebrows lurched. "Oh?"

"Saturday, Tuesday, Saturday, Tuesday."

"Meaning?"

"I figure they're running them someplace at least a day's drive away."

"They?"

"Seems likely there's more than one person involved."

"So you think they're selling them in, say, Oregon?"

Harland shook his head. "There's the border problem. It's tighter than ever. Most likely Alberta. Calgary? Maybe there's a drop point and they go farther east from there. Say, on to Quebec. Maybe gang related."

Angie frowned. "Maybe. But then there's a big yellow van with out-of-province plates. Kind of conspicuous."

"Stolen plates," said Harland. "Or two vans. No new theft for a few days, though; they've missed a Saturday and a Tuesday. So by now, maybe the van isn't yellow anymore."

Angie cocked her head to one side. "That had occurred to me, too. But I don't think they're hauling them east."

"To the coast, then?"

The receptionist stuck her head into the lunch room. "There you are, John. I've been buzzing your desk. You've got a woman waiting to see you."

"Sorry." Harland stood and drained his cup. "Send her to my desk, Misha. I'll be right there. Want your files back now, Angie?"

"I'll swing by in a bit and pick them up. Thanks for your thoughts."

"No problem." Harland set his mug in the sink and headed for his desk. He glanced across the office to the reception area, and felt a twinge of disappointment.

Clarissa Simms caught his eye, said something to the receptionist, then headed toward him. She held out her hand across the desk, and he shook it briefly before indicating the chair. Clarissa slid into the seat. Harland suspected that she was well aware that the normal buzz of the office had grown still, resuming abruptly only after she had swung her chair to face the desk, hiding her long legs from view.

"Thank you for coming in, Ms. Simms."

"Please, call me Clarissa." She propped her elbows on the desk and leaned forward conspiratorially. "I'm sorry I was out when you came by my house. What can I do for you?"

Harland opened his notebook. "I had a couple of questions I really should have asked you sooner. Ms. Simms— Clarissa—you said you last saw Mr. Hoskins on Friday night, when you dropped him off on Main Street?"

Clarissa sat back. "No, Constable Harland. I last saw him on Friday night, *and* I dropped him at Main Street."

Harland flipped his notebook. "Right. Did you see him after you dropped him off?"

"I did. At Jugs."

Clarissa watched Harland, and he wondered briefly if she was waiting for a particular reaction. He kept his tone neutral. "Do you recall what time that was?"

"Not long after I dropped him off." Clarissa shrugged.

"I drove straight over there, and he walked in a few minutes later."

"Do you think he had time to stop anywhere else?"

Clarissa shook her head. "I doubt it."

"Okay. Do you recall what Mr. Hoskins did when he arrived?"

"Yeah. He started whining about somebody being on his favorite stool. Then he headed in my direction."

"And you…"

"I ducked behind the guys I was with."

"And then?"

Clarissa smiled. "Wouldn't you know, Stan sits down at the table beside us."

"Did he speak to you?"

"No. He had his back to me. I don't think he saw me."

Harland jotted a couple of notes. "The guys you were with, who were they?"

Clarissa smiled at him. "Just a couple of the regulars. Not my type, but they ride nice bikes. Thought maybe one of them would offer to take me for a spin."

"Did they?"

"No. They were both crying in their beer about their bikes having been stolen. God, what a night. And it just kept getting better. I'm thinkin' it's time to blow this pop-stand when Stan up and decides he has to get into the conversation."

"Did he know the bikers?"

"Stan knows everyone and everything, to hear him tell it. That man is such an idiot."

Harland waited.

Clarissa clutched the edge of his desk and leaned toward him. "Look, this is not really… I mean, I… damn. Ellen is my best friend." She paused. "Here's the thing. Stan always *thinks* he *knows* stuff. Makes him feel big. So he tells these guys he knows where their bikes are. Right in the middle of Jugs. Like he figures he'll get some kind of reward for it."

"Reward?"

"Yeah." Clarissa's knuckles were white, and she released the desk, clasped her hands together. "Look. I go into Jugs now and again. You hear rumors, right? You don't know what's true, and what's not. So it's best to keep your mouth shut. But not Stan. He tells the guys the bikes are at a chop shop on Government and York. I mean, how stupid can he be?"

"Government and York?"

"Yeah. There's been rumors about that place for years. Probably started when somebody told the Jehovah Witnesses and the vacuum salesman to get lost in the same day; suddenly they gotta be up to something. Probably nothing going on there at all. But Stan, he makes a big deal about knowing what's happening, like he has some kind of inside line."

"Did the men—the bikers, did they appear to believe him?"

Clarissa rolled her eyes. "Nobody ever believes Stan. Besides, these guys know him. They work with him."

Harland stopped writing. "Both of them?"

"Yeah."

"Did anyone else hear this conversation?"

"Anyone nearby could have. Depends on who's yelling the loudest. It's a bar."

"Have you mentioned any of this to Mrs. Hoskins?"

Clarissa leaned back in her chair. "Like I said, Ellen's my friend. I sort of... well, I sort of ran it by her like it was a... a suggestion. That maybe Stan got himself in over his head, shot his mouth off once too often."

"Why didn't you just tell her what you heard?"

Clarissa was silent for a moment. "For years I've wanted to tell her some of the things I know about Stan."

Harland waited.

"Ellen is... she's very private. And she sees a lot of things differently. Like she makes the best of things, things most of us wouldn't stand for. She takes what she sees and paints a better picture, lives in her own little world. You can't just *wreck* her picture. You can't just come out and tell her something like 'Your husband's screwing around' or 'Stan might have been killed because he talks too much.' You can't."

Harland looked up from his notebook to find Clarissa watching him with narrowed eyes. "Did Stan speak to you at Jugs?"

Clarissa threw her head back and laughed, and every head in the office turned. "No," she said. "He didn't see me at first, and when he did, he pretended he didn't. Probably didn't want me to say how I'd found him earlier."

"And you?"

"I didn't want to have anything more to do with him, either. I got up and left."

"And you haven't seen him since?"

Clarissa's eyes flickered. She raised her chin. "No."

Harland closed his notebook. "Thank you for coming to see me, Ms. Simms."

"Clarissa." She stood.

Harland stood too, and shook the hand she offered across the desk. She clasped his hand a moment, looking directly at him. "You will be... kind with Ellen?"

"I will. Thank you again, Clarissa." Harland watched her go, then glanced over to Angie's desk. She raised her eyebrows. He shrugged at her, settled back into his chair, and ran his hand over his chin. It smelled like Clarissa's perfume.

ELEVEN

HARLAND COLLECTED the stack of files and stood. Angie had already crossed the room to perch on the corner of his desk.

She crossed her arms. "So. Tell me that was not the wife."

"The wife?"

"Your missing person file."

"Oh. No, she's not the wife." He smiled, and Angie's brow furrowed. Harland stopped smiling. "What's that look for?"

"Then she was the friend?"

Harland nodded. "Clarissa Simms. Fairly recently divorced, spending time in Jugs." He shook his head. "Doesn't really seem her kind of place."

"Ego boosting." Angie swung her foot in a circle. "Did she admit to being back to Jugs on the night your man Stan disappeared?"

"Oh yes. No problem with that. She was sitting with these two." He tapped the files. "Hoskins came in and sat nearby. Ms. Simms claims he told them their bikes could be found at a local chop shop."

"Really. He say which one?"

Harland flipped through his note book. "Government and York."

Angie whistled. "What did the guys say to that?"

"Ms. Simms left the bar at this point. From what I've been told, Stan did a lot of talking. People didn't usually believe him." He leaned back in his chair. "Angie, *is* there a chop shop on Government at York?"

"We've got some information to that effect. Had our eye on the place. There's a pretty serious fence around the property; but then, there's a lot of traffic on Government and a lot of residents use fencing to block the noise. There's a good sized garage in the back, accessible from the lane, well-locked. But that's true of half the homes in the neighborhood. Most of them were built when cement was cheap and cars were the size of tanks. And you'd be a fool not to keep things locked up these days."

"So nothing else?"

"Well, nothing concrete. The guy who owns the place is rumored to be unfriendly. Some of his neighbors have lodged complaints about his behavior; he yells at their kids, stuff like that. He has signs up; no soliciting, beware of dog. Might be he just like his privacy."

"Is there a dog?"

"Big one. Must weigh all of ten pounds, soaking wet."

"Maybe he just doesn't want anyone getting his dog riled. Wasn't that the area where that kid came onto the neighbor's property and whacked the dog with a stick and got bit, and the dog got put down for it?"

Angie nodded. "I remember that. The boy wasn't badly hurt. Owners insisted on a necropsy on the dog. Showed she'd taken quite a few whacks to the face."

"Dog was chained up, wasn't she?"

"Easy mark. Anyway, maybe this guy at Government and York just wants to be left alone. You figure out where he works?"

"He's on a disability pension of some kind. We haven't seen anyone come or go from the property except him. He pretty much just walks to the IGA and back. Bit of a recluse. Has something going in the shop out back; machining noises in the daytime. Shuts it down at night. Noise isn't a problem; no complaints from the neighbors in that department. Electrical consumption is a bit high, but a lot of those old places are badly insulated and most use electric heat." She shrugged. "Doesn't mean he's running a chop shop."

Harland fanned four of the files out. "You think that *is* what's happening to the Harleys, though?"

Angie smiled. "I do. Interesting. I've been keeping an eye on another property on Government, a couple of blocks from York." A city map hung on the wall, and she circled Harland's desk. He stood and joined her. She pointed to the intersection of Government and York. "This is the one Stan mentioned. We'll keep an eye on it, but I don't think he was right. This is the one we were watching." She slid her finger two blocks north along Government, to Warrick.

"On Warrick?" Harland asked.

"Not War-*ick*. Just *Wark*." Angie smiled. "Gotta pronounce it like you live here."

"So like York, with a W." Harland looked at Angie. "What if Stan did know something, after all?"

Angie shrugged. "Guess your Ms. Simms might have thought he said York, when he really said Warrick."

"Or he might have said York, and someone else thought he said Warrick. Bar's noisy."

Angie settled into the chair. "Did you notice the other connection between the Harleys?"

Harland glanced down at the files. "Just the Tuesday-Saturday thing. And daytime." He paused, looked across at Angie. "I missed something?"

"Check the stats on the owners."

Harland sat, taking the top file. "Andrew Flett, a.k.a. Helmet, born 1958, Moose Jaw Saskatchewan, resident of Penticton since 1962, currently 542 Archer Avenue. Separated. Currently employed by PenWest twelve years, no criminal record, few speeding tickets…"

"Next one," Angie interrupted.

"Arthur Jenkins, born 1961, resident of Penticton since 1985, currently 693 Perch Avenue. Divorced. Currently employed by PenWest three years, no…" Harland looked at Angie. She smiled. He opened the other two files, scanning them quickly. "Currently employed by PenWest eight years… PenWest, six months." He set the files down. "PenWest. Hell. Clarissa said something about that."

"Bit tough to concentrate on what that one's saying?"

He rolled his eyes. "Point is, somebody knew the owners would be at work."

"You got it."

"But then, wouldn't the guys start talking at work, lock their bikes up more securely?"

"Yes and no." Angie leaned forward, pointing to the files. "These owners aren't on the same shifts, and they aren't in the same part of the plant. One of them is in sales, one in management. Helmet and Jenkins are both in the shop, and there are about five different shop areas. Separate lunch rooms, different break times. PenWest is a big enough employer, these guys could have gone a few weeks without talking to each other. Except for these two; Helmet got his buddy Jenkins hired on there. The two of them go back a ways."

"But still. You'd think somebody would put two and two together, just reading the papers."

Angie shook her head. "Not necessarily. The general addresses are printed in the news stories—missing from eight-hundred block of Cooper—but the owners' names usually aren't. And certainly not their place of work."

"Okay. But Helmet and Jenkins."

"Well, now, they probably figure something's up," she agreed. "Jenkins' bike went second. Helmet's went last, from inside his locked garage. Carpet cleaner van was parked in the breezeway in front of the garage. The racket those things make covers any noise you'd make breaking into a garage. The thieves probably had the sound tape-recorded; there wouldn't be room in the van for the bike if they had cleaning equipment on board. So, nobody on the street would hear anything. Or see. Van covered the doorway. It's one of those old style, open-to-the-sides kind."

"So somebody knows the PenWest schedules, and home addresses." Harland opened a file: Lee Simmons. "Don't any of these owners have a roommate, spouse, common-law?"

"These two. Simmons and Lansing." Angie pointed to the files. "Both the spouses work most Saturdays. No children."

"So nobody around. Makes for easier planning."

"You bet."

"Any other employees at PenWest with bikes?"

"Seven."

Harland whistled. "You got all of them staked out?"

"Four of them are Harleys. We were concentrating on those."

"Were?"

"Yeah. One, the guy rides to work. It's a secure parking

lot there; pretty hard to steal that one in working hours. Second bike, there's a couple living in a suite downstairs. They're always home on Saturday. Party types—up late Friday and don't get mobile until way after lunch. We had stake-outs on the other two all day Saturday and Tuesday. Nothing."

"Spooked them?"

"Maybe. We're still doing drive-bys but we can't justify staking them out if there's no more action."

"How would you have spooked them? Talking to PenWest?"

Angie shook her head. "We don't think so. The only person we discussed this with was Lee Simmons—" she tapped the file Harland had open. "By the way, Lee's a 'she.' In management. She accessed the PenWest files we needed. She might have talked, but I don't think so."

"What day did she pull the files for you?"

"Wednesday, the day after the last bike was stolen." Angie shrugged. "Of course, it could be she was involved and tipped them off, but I doubt it. I figure the thieves got what they were after and wanted to lie low for a while, or something else spooked them. Maybe they spotted the stake-outs. Now I'm wondering if Hoskins had anything to do with it."

"With the thefts?" Harland rubbed his jaw. "You know he worked at PenWest, too."

"Did he, now." Angie's eyebrows settled into a frown. She crossed her arms. "Hoskins worked at PenWest, he was a busybody, he's missing. Think it's just coincidence?"

"Probably, but I'll look into it." Harland thought for a moment. What had Jack Allen implied? Hoskins had something on the manager, Peter Barry, something that kept him employed when he should have been fired. His admin assistant, Ms. Wilkins, hinted as much, too. Was Barry involved with the bikes, and Hoskins blackmailing him?

That didn't really click. The bikes were a new development. If Hoskins had anything on Barry, it went back years.

Unless Barry had recently added bike theft to something else he was involved with.

Harland shook his head. "More likely he knew—or *thought* he knew—something. Makes no sense he'd talk about it in the bar, not if he was actually involved."

Angie collected the files. "I think we'd better take this to the sergeant. Puts publicizing Hoskins' disappearance in a little different light. Maybe we can get him to keep it quiet a bit longer while we follow this up."

"I'm all for that." Harland pushed his chair under his desk. "It'll be a bit of good news for Mrs. Hoskins." He caught Angie giving him a look, and stopped short. "What?"

She was already through the sergeant's door.

Sergeant Macgregor looked up from his desk. "Good news, I hope?"

Angie plopped herself down in the chair across from him. "Not sure, Sarge. There does seem to be something of a tie-in between John's missing person and my stolen bikes."

Macgregor looked at Harland, who stood leaning against the doorframe. "Come in, Harland. That wall will stay up without your help." His attention was diverted to the reception area, where a small scuffle was erupting.

A scruffy-looking man leaned over the front counter. "You'll have to wait here to see an officer," Misha insisted, standing. "If you'll just have a seat, sir, I'll have someone see you as soon as possible." The man backed away, settling into the chair.

Misha picked up the phone, and the sergeant folded his arms and turned back to Harland.

"So. What's the connection?"

"The last we can place Mr. Hoskins, he was in Jugs, talking to the owners of two of the missing bikes."

"That's what you had earlier, Harland. So?"

"A witness, Ms. Clarissa Simms, claims Mr. Hoskins told them they could find their bikes at a local chop shop."

The sergeant frowned. "He say where the shop is?"

"Government and York."

Macgregor turned to Angie. "York? This something new?"

Angie shrugged. "Rumors, but nothing substantial. I don't think there's a chop shop there. We're actually wondering if there's some confusion between York and Warrick."

Macgregor nodded. "Sounds plausible."

"Plus, Hoskins works at PenWest. So do all the owners of the stolen Harleys."

"I see," said Macgregor. "You're hoping I'll sit on that media release?"

Angie nodded. "I think so. Hoskins usually walked home from Jugs, and I'd like to find out if his route would have taken him past Government and Warrick."

Macgregor stood and turned to the city map on the wall behind his desk. "Where'd he live?"

Harland pointed, and Macgregor traced southeast from Jugs. "Most likely came up Spencer, which ends in a cul-de-sac here, so he'd have taken the cut path through here, putting him into the alley behind Warrick. Takes you through to Knight's Park, right on Government."

"What do you think?" Angie asked.

Macgregor turned and dropped back into his chair. He reached for the photo of Stan. "This guy's been missing since when?"

"Saturday morning." The sergeant pushed the photo across the desk, scowling.

"Four days. Coming up on five. Wife must be wanting to see some kind of action."

Harland glanced at Angie. "I think she feels we're doing what we can."

Macgregor leaned back in his chair. "Doing what we can usually involves asking for the public's help."

Harland' ears reddened. "The wife—Mrs. Hoskins—is concerned about her husband, but not… ah… she's…"

Angie leaned forward. "Sarge, the man's a piece of work. Plus, turns out he's been tomming around. No woman in her right mind would want media involved at this point."

"I see." Macgregor looked up as Misha approached. "Yes?"

"Sorry to interrupt. There's a gentleman here who wants to report a murder."

Macgregor glanced skeptically at the derelict, who had returned to the counter. "That guy?"

Misha nodded.

"Can't someone else handle it until we're done here?"

"Schwartz was going to, but he thinks Harland will want it. The guy's a bit fuzzy on the details. Sounds like he sometimes sleeps in Knight's Park. Says that's where the murder happened, on the weekend." She turned to Harland. "Isn't that near when your missing guy disappeared?"

TWELVE

HARLAND WATCHED THE MAN stir four creamers and three packets of sugar into his coffee. The lunch room was deserted; most of the day staff had gone home already. Angie hovered discreetly near the doorway.

"Good coffee. Thanks." The man held the cup with both hands, as though his fingers were cold.

"So," said Harland, "the receptionist tells me you needed to speak with someone?"

"Indeed I do." The man looked from side to side, his long gray hair brushing the worn shoulders of his tweed jacket. He leaned forward. "It was murder."

Harland flipped open his notebook. "Murder?"

The man nodded solemnly. "Most foul."

"Pardon?"

"Murder most foul. As in the best it is. Hamlet. Act one, scene five, lines twenty-seven and -eight."

Harland glanced to the doorway to see Angie's eyebrows bounce. "Perhaps I should get your name and address, sir."

"Certainly. Certainly. Name's Will, sir. Will Shakespeare."

"Ah. And your address?"

"York, sir. I live in York. Seems wrong, yes, yet there it is. Ought to be London. Avon perhaps. But no; just York. At Government."

"You live on York?"

"Yes, yes. I suppose I do."

"At what number, Mr. Shakespeare?"

"Nine-oh-four." He looked at his coffee. "Nine-oh-four. There should be something there, some connection. Alas, no."

Angie had vanished.

Harland looked down at his notepad.

"So, Mr. Shakespeare. You want to report a murder?"

"Most foul."

"Yes. And where did this murder take place?"

The man sat back in his chair, tugging at his goatee. "In the wood."

"The wood?"

"The wood, a league without the town, where I did meet thee once with Helena. No, not yet a league. And 'twas within the town. A wood, nonetheless. A wood. The wood of the knights, though they call it now a park."

"A park. Oh. Knight's Park."

"Knight's Park. Where I wouldst go on a midsummer night's eve, there to sleep, perchance to dream of Helena. Fair Helena."

"You were... sleeping in the park that evening?"

He nodded. "To dream of Helena. But nay, 'twas not to be."

"What did you see?"

"I saw those of the house of Capulet as they set upon him."

"Upon whom?"

The man looked up, his piercing blue eyes staring directly into Harland's. "Hoskins. I saw them set upon the man called Hoskins. And then he was no more."

Angie returned to the doorway, and Harland looked up at her. The man turned in his chair, looking over his shoulder. "Ah, Kate." He stood and bowed.

"Good evening, Mr. Shakespeare. May I join you?"

"Certainly. Certainly." Pushing his empty cup aside, the man pulled out a chair.

Angie reached for Shakespeare's cup while sliding a piece of paper toward Harland. "More coffee?"

"'Twould be nice."

"Cream and sugar?"

"Four, and three."

"Here you go. John, coffee?"

"Please." Harland slid the paper into his notebook. In Angie's neat scrawl, it confirmed that a Mr. William Speare lived at 904 York Avenue, at the corner of Government. Beside the address she had written the words "chop shop," then crossed them out with an X.

He looked at her. "Mr. Shakespeare has been telling me about something he saw in Knight's Park a few nights ago."

Angie placed a cup of coffee in front of Harland and settled into a chair. "What night was this?"

Speare shook his head. "That isn't clear. Not clear at all. Methinks it ought to have been midsummer night, but that it could not have been." He stirred another creamer into his coffee. "Probably Friday."

"Friday night, in Knight's Park. You saw someone being killed?" Angie leaned toward him. "My goodness. Who?"

"Hoskins. Those of the house of Capulet got him. Set about him, they did, beating him about the head and shoulders. Murder. Most foul. After some time did those of Capulet leave, taking with them the spoils of their act. I watched. Then did I see his ghost rise up."

"Hoskins' ghost?" Angie's eyebrows skyrocketed.

"Aye. His ghost. With most unmartial stalk hath he gone by my watch. He did stagger, as with drink. From the northernmost edge of the wood did he cross within a hand's breadth of me, where I lay upon mine couch. With eyes unseeing, he passed me by, plodding on his painful way. He gained the roadway, to the south of the wood, weaving forth as would one crazed. Then didst the apparition vanish."

"It vanished?" Angie repeated.

"As swallowed by the earth. I didst cast my gaze hither and yon to see what had yet become of his earthly remains, and saw them not. I marveled." He sipped his coffee. "But then I didst see her, and then didst I understand."

Harland stopped writing. "Saw who?"

Speare shuddered. "I saw the Lady Macbeth."

HARLAND LOOKED AT ANGIE. She was nodding at William Speare, her expression solemn. "Lady Macbeth?"

Speare stirred another creamer into his coffee. "Gave me a fright, she did."

"Did she speak to you?"

"No, no. She saw me not. I stayed most still, reclining upon mine couch, and scarce didst breathe. She hovered at the northernmost edge of the wood, where moments before didst Hoskin's body lay a-cooling. And the ghost had vanished, so didst she."

"Into the earth?" asked Angie.

Speare shook his head. "Nay, good lady. She retired fleet into the darkness, beyond the lamp. Back to the north, whence had she come."

Angie leaned forward. "Mr. Shakespeare, I've never seen Lady Macbeth. Is she very beautiful?"

He frowned. "A frightening beauty, aye. Blood red lips, and yet more red her fingertips. And red even in the darkness of her long unplaited hair."

"You could see her beauty, even in the dark?"

"Nay, Kate. I couldst but see the shape, the flow of her, the stance. Yet did I recognize her, as I had seen her before, and since."

"Where else have you seen her?"

"Most oft in daytime, walking by the wood. I see her upon occasion when I go to market. Once didst we speak. 'Twas from her I learned the name of the man Hoskins. He had come upon me in repose upon my couch, and he didst hurl upon me invectives most vile. Most vile." Speare shook his head sadly, gazing into his coffee. He sighed. "Moments later, the lady didst say to me in passing," Speare stood, swept back his hair grandly and sang out in a sultry, feminine tone: "Don't mind him. Stan Hoskins is the meanest man who ever lived." He sank back into his chair and lowered his voice. "That day I didst not yet recognize who she was. Only last night didst I recognize that she is the Lady Macbeth."

Harland continued writing. "Last night?"

"She didst return to the wood. At first I thought her to be Cleopatra. She came and stood upon the place of the murder. She then proceeded to where the apparition vanished, and didst stand, and wring her hands. She lacked the season of all natures, sleep. And she didst wring her hands, and wring them more. Methinks she said, 'Yet here's a spot.' Then she spoke not." He drained his coffee. "Perhaps she had forgotten her lines."

"Her lines?" Angie refilled his cup.

"Out, damned spot." Speare opened a creamer. "Hell is murky... Macbeth, act five, scene one, lines thirty-three through thirty-eight. Who would have thought the old man to have had so much blood in him?"

"Ah, yes." Angie nodded. "The part in the play where Lady Macbeth went mad."

"Went mad?" Speare added a couple more sugar packets to his coffee. "Ma'am, Lady Macbeth was already mad at the beginning of the play. She just hadn't shown it yet. Sane people do not murder other human beings."

Angie blinked. "Of course you're right. Was the lady one of those who... set upon Mr. Hoskins?"

Speare shook his head. "No. She came along soon after. It was a man that killed Hoskins. A big man. That lady is quite tall, taller than most, but she's not that big."

"*One* man?" asked Harland.

"Yes. One big man. Came up behind Hoskins with something like a tire iron. Brought it down on his head, hard. Hoskins fell, and the man kicked him a couple of times. Kicked him hard. Then he left."

"Did you go over to where Mr. Hoskins lay?" Angie asked.

"I waited a bit to be sure the man was gone. I was about to get off the bench when Hoskins screamed."

"He screamed?"

Speare frowned. "Howled. Not unlike a cat did he scream. I have not forgot the taste of fears. My senses cool to hear a night shriek, and my fell of hair will at a dismal treatise rouse and stir as life were in't. 'Twas not the cry of women, nay. Hoskins didst cry out. Then his ghost didst rise and commence its walk. Then didst the Lady Macbeth appear, then didst she vanish."

"What did you do?"

"I didst wait but a moment, then didst I vanish as well."

"Did you go by the place where Mr. Hoskins was killed?"

"Nay, 'twould be a haunted place. As would the place his spirit lays. I didst take me home by a circuitous route, first east then south then west, far and far beyond the wood. I took me home, and thence to bed. To sleep. Perchance to dream." Speare stared into his coffee.

Harland looked at Angie, who raised her eyebrows only slightly. He turned back to Speare. "Well, Mr. Shakespeare. You have been quite helpful. May I call on you if I have any more questions?"

"Of course, Petruchio. And bring the good Kate with you." Speare rose and took Angie's hand. Bending as though to kiss it, he smiled into her eyes. "I thank you kindly for the drink, my lady."

"You are most welcome, Mr. Shakespeare. It was a pleasure to meet you."

Speare nodded to Harland, who closed his notebook. "I'll see you out, sir. Thanks again for bringing this to our attention."

"Aye. Good day, sir. Good day."

HARLAND WATCHED THOUGHTFULLY AS Speare strode away from the station. Angie appeared at his elbow. "What do you think?" he asked.

"Interesting character. I'd love to know what he does in that workshop all day." Angie smiled. "Do you think *anything* he said had any bearing on your case?"

"Or any basis in reality?" Harland smiled. "Hard to say. His description of Lady Macbeth remind you of anyone?"

Angie nodded. "Ms. Simms. Regal bearing; long, straight dark red hair."

"What do you make of her returning to the park?" He settled into his chair.

Angie perched on his desk. "If she did. Let's do away with all the Shakespearean stuff and look at the rest of what we've got. Speare says a man hit Hoskins over the head, kicked him repeatedly, and left him for dead. This happened at the north end of the park." She got up and pointed to the map. "Here's the north end, where the alley empties from the cul-de-sac to Warrick, then through to Chapman and then the park. Speare says that after a while Hoskins got up, staggered across the park, then vanished." She traced a line diagonally through the park to Government. "Then he saw the woman, back here."

Harland pointed to a spot about halfway between Warrick and Chapman. "Clarissa Simms lives here."

Angie whistled. "Think she had something to do with the guy that beat Hoskins up?"

Harland shook his head. "Hard to say. But let's say she sees Stan staggering through the alley."

"Drunk?"

"Maybe not. He got to Jugs pretty close to closing time. So let's say he's walking home through the back lane, and Simms sees him. Then she sees the other guy."

"Who's the other guy?"

Harland slid his finger half a block north. "If it's the guy from your chop shop on Warrick and Government, the alley took Stan right past his back yard."

"So let's say it's him, and he's following Hoskins. Does Simms recognize him?"

"Maybe. Probably. They live half a block apart. Say she watches him go by, sees him come back a couple of minutes later, then hears Hoskins—Speare said he screamed?"

"Yeah." Angie shook her head. "Wouldn't that have gotten the neighbors looking?"

"Wee hours, and Speare said he screamed like a cat."

"Mmm. He might have said that to make it work with Macbeth. Fits with the witches' bit, 'double, double, toil and trouble,' all that jazz. There's a line in there somewhere about the scream of a cat. But you're right; if the neighbors thought it was a tomcat, they wouldn't have paid much attention."

"Plus, Speare says he screamed, then got up and headed across the park and disappeared, and *then* the woman showed up. Not much time for neighbors to wake up, get involved."

"True." Angie frowned. "So Hoskins is in bad shape, maybe drunk, maybe disoriented from the blow to the head. He staggers across the park to Government, and he vanishes. Disappears. Swallowed up by the earth. Swallowed up..." She traced her finger along Government. "John, was the storm sewer project still underway when Hoskins disappeared?"

ACT III

THIRTEEN

ELLEN AWOKE WITH A START. She stared at the empty pillow beside her head. Moments before, Stan's head had rested there, bandaged and bloody. She had watched from above, her body suspended against the ceiling. Stan's eyelids had fluttered, then he'd glared up at her. His mouth opened, and dirt poured out.

"You owe me, Ellen," he snarled.

She shook her head, grabbed her robe. The clock beside the bed said 2:49. Stan had been dead five days and, approximately, four minutes.

Monte thumped his tail as Ellen entered the kitchen. Moonlight streamed through the window, and she left the lights off.

Filling the kettle, she looked at the darkened windows next door. Jason had come by for a romp with Monte after school, and when he collected the recipe card he repeated his invitation to come over and meet his mom. Ellen wondered if his mother was truly interested in meeting her. It would have been nice to just say 'hi' over the fence a few times first.

The kettle boiled and shut itself off, its shrill whistle softening into a melancholy moan. Ellen stood gazing out into the dark. In the porch, Monte sat up, watching her. He whined softly, and finally she turned. "It's okay, boy." She came to pat him, rubbing his ears absent-mindedly until he settled against the door. "It's okay."

Of course, it was not okay. There would be no more peace. Constable Harland had come by in the evening, this time accompanied by another officer, Constable Angie Wilson. She seemed a combination of motherly concern and hard-nosed cop, and Ellen had been uncomfortably aware during their entire stay that Constable Wilson was sizing her up.

Harland was also uncomfortable. They had come with bad news: the sergeant wanted to go to the media tomorrow, but in the meantime, a witness had come forward who claimed that Stan had been beaten senseless, if not to death, at the edge of Knight's Park.

Ellen had sat, stunned into silence. Constable Wilson had added that the witness wasn't someone entirely reliable, but his description of the events may have been accurate.

Ellen couldn't think what to say.

Did she want them to call someone? Perhaps Ms. Simms?

She shook her head. No; Clarissa is on evening shift. Thank you for coming. I'd like to be alone now. Goodbye.

Shell shock. Like when Robbie died. Gray haze. Limbs like lead. Eyelids, too; impossible to keep them open. Impossible to think. Impossible.

Undressing on autopilot, she'd fallen into bed, escaped into sleep.

Monte leaned against her, and she stroked his head. Someone might have seen… something. What?

Someone saw someone beating Stan to death.

That didn't make sense.

Or maybe it did.

Ellen put her face in her hands and wept.

THE MORNING SUN WARMED Ellen's arms as she rinsed the breakfast dishes. The back gate clicked shut, and she turned to see Clarissa cross the yard.

Clarissa knocked, then swung the door open. "Just me." She kicked off her sandals, and stood in the doorway. "Thought I'd join you and Monte for a walk, if you haven't already... Oh, my god, Ellen. You look like hell. What's happened?"

Ellen's throat tightened, and she turned back to the sink, shaking her head.

"Damn, what a stupid question. Honey, it's all catching up with you, isn't it?" Clarissa put her hands on Ellen's shoulders and turned her around. "Come here, girl. Even you need a hug sometimes. Give it up."

Ellen sagged against her, tears rolling.

Clarissa held her. "Atta girl, you just let it go. It's going to be alright, Ellie. You'll see."

Ellen shook her head. "The cops... came by."

Clarissa stiffened. "News?"

Ellen nodded.

"What?" Clarissa pulled Ellen down onto a chair. She reached for the tissue box and plunked it down on the table. "It's okay, El. Take your time."

Ellen blew her nose, wiped her eyes. Clarissa settled into the chair beside her, leaning over to rub her back.

"They think... they think they have a witness."

Clarissa's hand stilled. "A witness?"

Ellen nodded, staring down at the wet tissue.

"El, a witness to what?"

"They say someone... someone came forward... someone they're not sure they can... they can believe. This person says... they say... Clarissa, they think Stan might have been beaten to death."

Clarissa's breath sucked in, and she sat back in her chair. "Oh my god."

Ellen pulled another tissue from the box.

"Did they say where this happened?"

Ellen nodded. "Knight's Park. Where the alley comes out from behind Government, from behind your place." She twisted the tissue. "On his way home from Jugs. He was there, after all."

"After all?"

Ellen swallowed, lumping the tissue into a ball. "I didn't think he had been. I called, Saturday afternoon, and they said no. But I guess now somebody's saying he was there. Near closing time."

Clarissa leaned over to put her hand on Ellen's arm. "He was there, Ellen. I saw him at Jugs a little while after I dropped him at Main Street. I'm sorry... I didn't realize you didn't know."

Ellen swallowed again, then looked up. "Clarissa, that... that little story about... about the chop shop. Stan blabbing. Was that... was that true?"

"God." Clarissa sighed, sat back in her chair. "Ellen, promise you won't hate me?"

Ellen stared at her.

Clarissa bit her lip. "Ellen, I want you to know that I... you're... I didn't want to hurt you. But I..."

"You what?"

"I... I think I know what happened to Stan."

They stared at each other in silence for a moment, then Clarissa stood, reached for a tissue and ducked into the porch, her shoulders heaving.

Ellen felt as though she were made of stone. Clarissa blew her nose, bent to pat Monte, then sagged into the chair across from Ellen. "It wasn't just a story. He did tell the bikers about the chop shop. Only, he had it wrong. He said Government and York. But that guy that lives a couple houses up the road from me... the guy from the corner of Warrick? I think people call him Franco. He was sitting behind Stan."

Ellen waited.

"I was getting ready for bed when I saw Stan go by, through the back lane. You know how my bathroom faces out that way, and my neighbor's security light picks up when somebody's moving around back there? Anyway, it came on and whoever tripped it was just about past the lighted up area, and I had the impression it was Stan, but I didn't really pay any attention except now the light was on and I saw this Franco guy coming along the alley, kind of dodging in and out of back gates, like maybe he's following the first guy, and that's when I get this feeling like... like something really bad is going to happen." She blew her nose.

"And..."

"Well, so I go into the back yard, think I'll have a smoke while I think what to do, maybe follow him and make some noise. Scare the guy off. But I'm too scared. I don't want to get involved. And then I see Franco coming back again. He's got something in each hand, and he's still dodging around sneaky, like he's trying not to be seen, but of course that damn security light comes back on and now I'm sure it's him and he stops right outside my gate for a moment and I wonder if he can see me and I think my heart's pounding so loud I'm sure he'll hear it. And then, from over toward the park, I hear this..." Clarissa put her hands to her ears.

"What did you hear?"

Clarissa flinched. "I heard this scream."

"What did you do?"

Clarissa put her hands over her face. "I just stood there until Franco was gone and I'd heard his gate slide shut, back up his end of the alley, and then I headed to the edge of the park. And I saw..."

"What? Clarissa, what did you see?"

"I saw a man fall into the ditch."

"The ditch?"

"Yeah. That ditch they'd made for the storm drains. It was still dug up at the time."

Ellen took a breath. "Then what did you do?"

"I... I..."

"You what?"

"God forgive me, Ellen... I went home."

Ellen watched Clarissa crumple onto the table, sobbing. Finally, she stood and gathered Clarissa against her chest.

Clarissa clutched Ellen's arms, still sobbing, the back of her head jerking under Ellen's chin. "Ellen, I don't know what got into me. It was horrible of me, I know. I thought... I thought, *good, he's gone.* And I went home. And I got ready for bed. And then I went to bed. And I lay there, thinking about... thinking about him just... just lying there, maybe bleeding to death, maybe dying, and... and I couldn't sleep. So finally, I got up and... and I went back."

Ellen stiffened. "You went back? To the ditch?"

Clarissa nodded. "Yeah... and I took a flashlight. And my cell phone. And I went in my car. Because I thought... I thought... what if that Franco comes back to finish him off? What if I end up in the ditch with Stan?"

"Clarissa, why didn't you just call the police?"

"Because... I didn't want to explain why I didn't call them right away and... and what if he was dead now, and it was... it was because I didn't help him." Clarissa collapsed into a fresh burst of tears.

Ellen crouched on the floor beside her, stroking her arm. "Clarissa, it's not your fault. You didn't do anything."

"I should have done something!"

"It was dark. Do you even know for sure it was Stan?"

Clarissa shook her head. "Well, I was pretty sure. He had that walk... But when I got back there, he was gone."

"You mean the ditch was empty?"

"Yeah. No sign of anybody having been in it at all. Ellie, I'm sorry. I'm so sorry."

Ellen handed Clarissa a fresh tissue. "Clarissa, it's not your fault. Besides, it might not even have been Stan. Could have been some other guy who just climbed out of the ditch and went home. And that guy—that Franco—he might not have had anything to do with Stan. Are you sure the guy you saw didn't just jump into the ditch? Maybe because he saw you coming?"

Clarissa blew her nose. "Well, maybe."

"If this Franco is involved with something illegal, maybe he was meeting some guy in the park about it. Like a drug deal, trading cash for drugs. Maybe the guy saw you coming and jumped into the ditch to hide, then climbed out when you left."

Clarissa blew her nose again. "Yeah. Maybe. But what about the scream?"

"Are you sure you heard a scream? If you did, how come nobody else showed up to see what was going on?"

Clarissa frowned. "Well, it was late, and I guess it wasn't very loud. Maybe I just heard it because I was outside."

"But are you sure you didn't just hear an animal or something?"

"Maybe." Clarissa shrugged. "Or maybe it was a scream and it had nothing to do with Franco, or Stan, or the guy in the ditch. But you said the cops have a witness who saw something."

"Even if they do, and even if what they're saying is true, that doesn't mean you did anything wrong. Look, Clarissa, what if you had gone over to the ditch, and some guy that was involved with Franco... what if you got..." Ellen pulled Clarissa against her again. "Clarissa, if Stan's gone, he's gone. But what if I lost you, too?"

Clarissa clung to Ellen's arms. "I should have told you."

Ellen groaned. "Clarissa, you never want to tell me anything painful. Am I that hard to talk to?"

"No." Clarissa sniffed, turned to look up at her. "It's

just, you've had so much shit in your life already. I don't want to bring more into it."

Ellen squeezed her shoulder, then settled into a chair. "Clarissa, it's easier to get bad news in the privacy of my own home and from someone who cares about me than it is to get it from a stranger. If you know stuff I need to know, *tell* me. You're my friend. It's your job."

"A weighty responsibility, El." Clarissa smiled weakly. "Besides, if the good Constable Harland had his way, he wouldn't be such a stranger."

Ellen rolled her eyes. "Clarissa, you're incorrigible."

"I'm in *what?*"

"Never mind. Oh, Monte. Poor boy, are we ignoring you?"

Monte's tail beat a rapid tattoo against the door.

Clarissa wiped her face. "I was going to join you for a walk, but I don't think I want to head out in broad daylight looking like this."

Ellen smiled. "Monte and I went out really early, for the same reason. I almost wore sunglasses, but I thought it would look pretty silly. No one was around. Except Mr. Shakespeare. I don't think he ever sleeps. You met him?"

"The guy in the weird old-fashioned clothes that sits in the park in the evenings and quotes stuff?"

Ellen nodded. "All his life's a stage, literally. Right now he thinks I'm Desdemona."

"Desda-who?"

"From Othello. Desdemona. Her husband kills her in a fit of jealous rage."

"Oh. Sounds quite pleasant. So is that guy's name really Shakespeare?"

Ellen shrugged. "He certainly thinks so. He's actually quite nice. Lives on Government. Monte and I talk to him now and again."

"But he's at least a little bit deranged. Don't be over there by yourself, Ellen."

Ellen shook her head. "He's harmless. Just a bit lonely."

Clarissa rolled her eyes. "My god. You do collect lame ducks, don't you? How's the boy next door?"

"Jason? I'm to meet his mother tomorrow for coffee, although I'm not sure how she feels about that. Poor woman works two jobs and always seems exhausted."

"Ah, another lame duck. The two of you should be fast friends in no time." Clarissa scowled. "What's my weakness, Ellie? How come you're friends with me?"

"Weakness?" Ellen laughed. "Clarissa, you're the strongest woman I know."

Outside, a door slammed, and Monte leaped up, whining expectantly. Ellen let him out, glancing at the clock. "That'll be Jason, on his way to school. Clarissa, when's the last time you had peanut butter and banana pancakes for breakfast?"

"Peanut butter and banana pancakes? Are you kidding me? Sounds disgusting."

"Well, my girl, you haven't lived." Ellen reached for her recipe box. "Go have a smoke, and brace yourself. It's time for an adventure."

FOURTEEN

MISHA HELD OUT a handful of pink message papers. "Morning, John. The sergeant wants you in his office."

"Thanks, Misha." Harland glanced down at the notes. "Angie in yet?"

"She's in there with him."

Harland nodded. He tossed his jacket onto his chair and headed to Macgregor's office.

"Morning, Harland. Or is it Petruchio, now? Glad you could join us today. Close the door behind you."

Angie grinned.

"So. Kate here has been filling me in on your latest. You talk to the Simms woman yet?"

Harland pulled out the chair next to Angie's and sat facing Macgregor. "She wasn't home, but I've left word that I'd like to speak with her." He flipped open his notebook. "I did get hold of the city works department, though; the ditching alongside Knight's Park was the last section of the storm drain that was still open Friday night. They filled it in on Saturday morning."

"Public works, putting in time on a Saturday?"

"Contractors, I think. Something about the equipment being needed elsewhere on Monday."

Macgregor scowled. "How would anybody fall in? I was by there when it was dug up. Don't they leave the dirt piled on one side, and a barricade on the other?"

Harland shook his head. "This last block, they didn't have any dirt piled up. Those ditches were pretty deep, and they couldn't place all the dirt on the street without narrowing it too much for traffic. They hauled a lot of the dirt to a holding field, then trucked it back when the pipes were in. The day before, they had some kind of equipment shortage, so they used a loader to haul the dirt from the park block instead."

"Meaning?"

"Meaning there was no dirt piled up alongside the ditch that night to act as a barricade."

Angie's eyebrows bounced. "So surely they put up more barricades—sawhorses, something, right?"

"They did," said Harland. "Sometime during the night, somebody took them up Carmi, set them up to direct traffic to a bush party. One of our patrols picked them up at around oh-four-thirty, returned them to the work site."

Macgregor grunted. "Still, it's alongside a park. There are streetlights?"

Angie leaned forward. "That's the section of Government that people are petitioning about. Nearest light doesn't work, and the next one is more than a block away. There's just the one at the end of the alley. Apparently it only works intermittently."

"So your Mr. Speare could have been telling the truth."

"After a fashion," said Angie. "John, did you ask them if there was any chance they could have filled in over a body?"

Harland nodded. "I asked. There's no way. If Hoskins did fall into the ditch, he was out again by morning."

"Any sign somebody had been in there?" Macgregor asked.

"Nothing they noticed. They inspect the ditches before they fill them, make sure no critters got in overnight, nothing in the pipes that'll cause them grief later." Harland shrugged. "Mind you, the guy I was talking to did get a little evasive when I asked whether or not they always climb right down into the ditches for a good look. Someone may have been in there during the night, but by the time the work crew got there, the ditch was definitely empty."

Macgregor picked up the photo of Hoskins, grimacing. "Well, this is a problem, isn't it? We've got this guy missing since Saturday morning, and here it's Thursday and we've not been seen out pounding the pavement. Search and Rescue hasn't been called in. No media release requesting the public's help. Time to shake things up."

Angie leaned forward. "I was hoping to poke around at the chop shop first."

"*Alleged* chop shop. Angie, you think this is tied in somehow with your bikes, and I can agree that there's a possibility. But you know you can't get a warrant based on this Speare guy's testimony. Go over there and ask a few questions, though. That Franco guy was in Jugs the night Hoskins disappeared. Maybe he talked to him. Take Petruchio here with you, and do it right away. This will hit the news at noon."

Angie and Harland stood to leave. Macgregor tossed the photo on top of the file. "It would be nice to keep this off the TV. People always go off the deep end when somebody disappears. Harland, let me know if the Simms woman can corroborate Speare's story."

Harland checked his messages, then joined Angie as she headed out of the building. "Nothing new. I was hoping Ms. Simms had called back. Hey, Angie, who is this Petruchio character?"

"Taming of the Shrew. Petruchio bets he can tame the shrew—a crusty young woman, Kate. He wins the bet—and her, of course. Now that she's in love with him, she's putty in his hands."

"Sounds a bit politically incorrect."

"Rather." They had arrived at the passenger side of the cruiser, and Angie unlocked the door and passed Harland the keys. "Would you please drive today, John? I want to look over my notes on the way there."

HARLAND PARKED BESIDE A TALL, forbidding fence on Warrick. They walked east to Government and approached the front of the house. "You want to do the talking?"

"Yeah," said Angie. As she opened the gate, barking erupted behind the house and grew louder as a black and tan dog bounded into the front yard. Angie pulled the gate closed, peering over the fence at the nervous animal. "What do you think, John?"

"He's certainly doing his job." Harland considered presenting his hand for the dog to sniff, took a closer look at the bared teeth, and changed his mind.

"Jake, come!" The dog whirled toward the door of the house. A tall man stood in the doorway, arms folded across his muscular chest, framing the big-breasted girl on his faded t-shirt. "Can I help you?"

"Good morning," said Angie, her hand still on the gate latch. "We're hoping so. May we come in?"

"Sure. Jake'll be fine now I'm here."

Harland closed the gate, looking around the tidy yard. Like most in the neighborhood, it was small with a compact house, and a larger back yard accessible from the alley.

Angie had reached the steps. "I'm Constable Angie

Wilson, this is Constable John Harland. Are you Franklin Anderson?"

"Yeah. What's up?"

"We've been told you were in Jugs on Friday night. We're hoping you may have spoken to Mr. Stan Hoskins." Angie held out a copy of the photo. "Do you remember seeing him in Jugs that night?"

Franco frowned, scratching his dark beard. "Stan. Lemme see, Friday... yeah, I prob'ly saw him there, alright. Never spoke to him, though."

"Is he a friend of yours?"

"Nope. He in some kinda trouble?"

Angie put the photocopy back in her file. "We're trying to locate him. He's been missing since that night at Jugs."

Franco's eyes widened. "Missing. I ain't heard nothin' about it on the news."

"Well, we're still trying to determine whether or not Mr. Hoskins has disappeared of his own accord. Do you recall who he was speaking with on Friday night?"

"Geez. Lemme think." Franco glanced over at Jake, who was sitting at Harland's feet getting his ears rubbed. He scowled. "Hoskins was sittin' behind me. Can't say I seen him talk to anybody."

"We've been told that at some point, he spoke with Helmet and Jenkins."

Franco frowned again, nodding. "Yeah. Yeah, now that you mention them, I do recall him talkin' to them."

Angie waited a moment. "Were you able to hear any of the conversation?"

"Not that I recall."

"We've also been told that he was seen coming home through the alley behind this block. Mind if we have a look around back there?"

Franco smiled. "Sure, no problem. Come on around. You folks lookin' for anything in partic'lar?"

"Nothing in particular. Nice big shop you have back here."

"It's a beauty," said Franco, pulling keys from his pocket. "You need me to unlock it?"

"Would it have been locked on Friday night?"

"It's always locked. Got a lot of real valuable tools in there." He turned to Harland. "Wanna see?"

"Sure," he said. "Wood shop?"

"Nope." Franco snapped open the padlock, then pulled back two bolts. He entered the shop, and reached for the switch. Several rows of fluorescent lights flickered to life.

Five Harley Davidson motorcycles stood neatly lined up. A sixth was in parts, spread across a set of shelving that ran up the wall alongside the work bench. The gas tank cover was masked, and the fairing sported yellow flames. The smell of paint was strong in the air.

Angie walked over to one of the bikes. "Nice panhead. I haven't seen this one on the road for a while. Used to belong to that guy in Summerland—Kocinski?"

"Still does. I'm storin' it for him."

"How about these others? They yours?"

Franco shook his head. "Storin' 'em all for friends."

"Storing and repairs." Harland nodded at the tool chests that lined the wall. "Doing a little back-yarding on the side?"

"Oh, no. Nothin' like that," said Franco. "Just favors for friends."

"Ah." Harland nodded. "Sounds like you'd be a good friend to have in your corner." He looked at the back door of the shop, which opened garage-style onto the alley. It was bolted to the floor with three heavy, padlocked chains. The power cord for the automatic opening system was unplugged. A single shop window was placed high in the wall, and it had been painted over and covered with security grating from the inside and out. "Lot of trouble with break-ins in this area?"

"Some. Not here, not since I got Jake." The dog looked up from where he was gnawing on a piece of rawhide, then resumed chewing.

Harland smiled. "Did Jake act like anything unusual was happening on Friday night?"

Franco frowned, rubbed his beard. "Nope, nothing I can recall."

"Anyone else live here?"

"Nah. Just me and Jake."

"Mind if I poke around behind your back fence?"

"Course not. I'll hang around back here, tell Jake it's okay."

Angie had finished her inspection of the bikes. "Well, your friends sure have some beauties. Thanks for your time, Mr. Anderson. Can we catch you at home later if we have anything further?"

Franco shrugged carelessly. "Sure. Call first." He smiled. "Jake won't let you in the yard, and if I don't hear him bark I won't know you're here. Number's in the book." He locked the shop.

"Okay. We'll check the lane now. Thanks again."

A search of the back alley yielded little. Two empty garbage cans lay on their sides behind Franco's shop, and a small pile of bricks leaned against the fence. Angie lifted one of the bricks, creating pandemonium among the ants that had built their home beneath it. "These have been here a while," she said. "See anything?"

"Not much." Harland bent to examine the ground in front of the garage door. The gravel had recently been raked, and not a single tire track disturbed its surface. He pointed to the frame of the garage door. It sported a coat of fresh yellow paint.

They moved toward the corner of the garage. "Well, thanks again, Mr. Anderson," said Angie. "We'll be continuing down the alley toward the park. Might call in on our way back."

"No problem," he said. "I'll be here a while."

Empty garbage cans lined the alley. The yards were all fenced, some with chain link and some with wood, all in various states of disrepair. Three doors down from Franco's,

Harland paused. "This would be Ms. Simms' backyard. I may as well see if she's home."

Angie waited by the gate as he crossed to the door. The yard was an interesting jumble of plants and yard-sale finds—pieces of pottery, some broken and half buried, others intact perched on aging metal stands; an old watering can, half-buried at an artistic angle, vines spilling from its rusting spout. A hammock dangled between the fence and an ancient oak tree, and just inside the gate a couple of chairs were tucked invitingly into a vine-covered arbor.

His knock went unanswered. Returning to the gate, he surveyed the neighboring property. A small shed sported a security light, aimed into the side yard and angled to catch motion from the back fence. Angie poking around in the neighbor's hedge. He circled around her and started checking behind the next yard. "Angie, we should probably be doing a full-scale search of this area, talk to the residents."

"You're right, but I just wanted to do a quick check while we're here. We've already missed garbage pick-up." A small apartment building sat at the end of the block, and Angie pulled herself up to peer into the dumpster. "Good news. This hasn't been emptied for a while." She pulled her radio from its holster.

While Angie called the office, Harland checked the thick metal bar that spanned two posts at the end of the alley, blocking traffic from entering the park. Its padlock was securely in place. The post on one side completed a long stretch of tall chain link fence that surrounded the park, and an ancient lamp leaned precariously from its top. The next stiff wind should bring it crashing down.

A three-foot gap between the post and the apartment building's wooden fence allowed pedestrian and pedal traffic through. Harland squatted and peered at the post. "Hey, Angie. We'll want forensics down here. Look at this."

Angie leaned down beside him. He pointed to a dark smear about a foot off the ground, and a similar, less distinct one about a foot and a half higher.

"Blood?" he suggested.

"Could be." Angie straightened. "If Stan was attacked and he dropped here, he might have pulled himself up using the post." She looked upward, turning in a circle. "Great spot for an ambush. Nearest street light is on the other side of the apartment building, if this one's out. And this is the only way in or out of the park on this side."

Harland nodded. "There's the bench. Wait here a minute. Let's see if Speare's story makes any sense."

A path of stamped asphalt wound through the lawn. It split at the bench, one branch leading to the sidewalk on Government, the other toward a playground in the middle of the park. The bench sat along the curve of the path, facing northeast. Harland lay down on it with his head at the north end. He had a good view of the grocery store across the street, and the apartment building, but unless he craned his neck back he couldn't see Angie at all.

Swiveling around, he tried with his head to the south. Now Angie was plainly in view. His eyes followed the line of the path, and by tilting his head slightly he could see where it joined the sidewalk.

He stood and walked to the street.

Angie joined him. "Well?"

"Pans out. So far Mr. Speare's story seems like it could be rooted in fact."

Angie turned back toward the apartments. "Might as well check out the other side of the alley while we wait for the crew to show up."

FIFTEEN

"IT WAS NICE TO SEE YOU AGAIN, Constable Harland." Clarissa stood to leave.

Harland stood too, and walked her to the reception gate.

"You will call us if you think of anything else that might be remotely useful?"

"Of course." She smiled, and left.

Angie waved him over to her desk. "Looks like some of the wind has gone out of her sails. What did she have to say?"

Harland sighed. "She pretty much backed up what Speare told us. Too bad she didn't come forward with this sooner."

"Why didn't she?"

"Says she wasn't a hundred percent sure it was Hoskins. She still isn't."

"Sarge wants to see us." She stood. "Fill us both in."

"Come in." Macgregor hung up his phone. "I was on hold, anyway. So. Was Ms. Simms at the park that night?"

Harland nodded. "She came as far as the fence at the end of her back alley."

"Why?"

"Says she saw someone go by, in the lane. Security light over at the neighbor's came on while she was brushing her teeth."

"She see who it was?"

"Says she had the impression it was Hoskins, but maybe just because he usually goes home that way, and he would have been walking by at about that time. Anyway, light went on, she looked up, whoever was there was already pretty much behind her vines. A few seconds later, she saw Franco—Franklin Anderson—head toward the park."

Angie raised her eyebrows. "She wasn't sure the first guy was Hoskins, but she was sure the second guy was Franco?"

"Light was already on, so she'd have noticed the movement sooner, paid more attention."

Macgregor shrugged. "Makes sense."

Harland flipped through his notes. "Says she 'got a bad feeling, with Franco having been in the bar and Stan shooting off his mouth'. Says she went outside thinking she'd 'make some noise to spook Franco, but got too creeped out.'

Then she sees Franco is heading for home, walking 'like he doesn't want to be seen.' Thinks he might have been carrying something, too. She waits a bit for him to get into his yard, thinking she'll go have a look at the park. Then she hears a scream."

Macgregor cocked his head to one side. "So. She's out in the dark, she's creeped out, and she hears a scream. She doesn't think to call the police?"

Harland shook his head. "Says she headed down the alley to see what was up."

"Right." Macgregor snorted. "Doesn't sound likely, her being a woman and all."

Angie smiled serenely. "From what I've seen of Clarissa, I'm betting she's a very confident, get-things-handled kinda gal."

Macgregor frowned at her. "You would have gone to check it out?"

"Of course. Just like you would have."

Macgregor shrugged. "Okay, maybe. So, what does she see?"

Harland glanced down at his notes again. "Somebody across the park on the sidewalk at Government. Whoever it was disappeared into the ditch."

"Fell in?" asked Angie.

"Or jumped. Her impression was that he fell in."

Macgregor grunted. "So, now does she get help?"

Harland shook his head. Ms. Simms had been careful in this part of her statement, and he scanned his notebook for her exact words. "I thought it was probably Stan, and he was probably drunk and fell in the ditch, and I thought spending the night there would do him good." He looked up from the notebook. "Says she went home to bed."

"What? She just leaves some guy out there in the rain, at the bottom of the ditch?"

Angie smiled. "Yeah, but Sarge, at this point, she figures it's Hoskins, and from what we've heard, most people who knew him would have done just that."

"It wasn't raining yet," said Harland. "Anyway, Ms. Simms says she started wondering if it really was Hoskins, or if someone else was lying injured at the bottom of the ditch. She went back, but this time in her car, with a flashlight and her cell phone. There was no sign of anybody in the ditch."

Macgregor leaned his arms on the desk. "She say what time this was?"

Harland checked his notes. "Around three-thirty."

"Great. Now we see him, now we don't. So her story pretty much corroborates Speare's."

"And Speare was sure it was Hoskins." Angie shrugged. "Sounds to me like it all pans out."

Macgregor scowled. "So why didn't Ms. Simms tell you any of this earlier?"

Harland shrugged. "Says she wasn't really sure what she saw, and that she was ashamed of herself for not seeing if he was okay."

"You buy that?" asked Macgregor.

"I don't know."

"In her other statements, she withheld information. Did she actually lie?"

"No. The guy that went into the ditch was probably involved with Franco. He's not a guy she'd want to mess with, so why should she stick her neck out?" Harland closed his notebook. "Angie filled you in about what we found at his place?"

"Been on the phone." Macgregor sat back in his chair. "I hear forensics got called out."

"Yeah," said Angie. "To the alley. Nothing useful in the dumpster, but we found some blood. It's at the lab."

"Anything at the alleged chop shop?"

Angie smiled. "Lots of bikes."

Macgregor tilted his head. "Harleys?"

"Yeah. In storage, for friends. All local to the area. I know the owners of most of them. We're running the plates now. One bike was being repainted."

"So. What do you think?"

"Phony as all get out, Sarge. Nobody stores their bikes at this time of the year; it's riding season. Okay, two of them aren't insured. Maybe a couple people can't afford to get them on the road yet. But five?" She shook her head. "It stinks. He's got the tools and the technology for a chop shop. Says he's doing favors for friends, fixing up their bikes."

"Back-yarding without a business license?"

Angie shook her head. "Nope. I think that's what he *wants* us to think. Only time he acted nervous was when Harland here suggested that's what he was up to, and I think he was faking it. The whole set-up reeked. His shop was a little too tidy, a little too perfect. Plus, he was real anxious to show us what he had in there."

"You figure he got spooked, called up some friends and had them haul over their bikes to make things look legit?"

Angie frowned. "That's where things don't really work. I'm not sure I believe that he'd have a lot of friends with bikes if he's known for stealing and chopping them."

"Anything else?"

"Fresh yellow paint on the frame of the garage door."

"So?"

"So the van was yellow, the one that was seen at three of the four theft sites." She glanced at Harland. "John figures someone was careless, scraped the wall on the way in or out."

"Maybe he's just touching up."

"Maybe. But the yellow doesn't really work with the green exterior, and the rest of the trim is white."

"So, like you say, it stinks."

Angie nodded. "Like fresh paint. And pot."

"Pot?"

"Yeah. I couldn't be sure at first with fresh paint inside and out. But it's there. He's had a grow-op in that garage."

"Grow-op *and* chop shop?"

"Seasonal, maybe." Angie grinned. "Chop shop pot

crop—say that five times, fast. Maybe those bikes belong to his loyal customers."

Macgregor nodded. "He calls them up, says the cops are coming around and he needs to pull the plants and replace them with bikes. Plausible, but that's a big assumption on smell alone."

"But it wasn't just the smell," said Harland. "There were also those shelves. The ones the bike parts were on. They're usually not stacked, and they're usually rigged with fluorescent lights and drip irrigation."

Angie cocked her head. "I missed that."

Harland nodded. "You were checking out the bikes. There's an automatic irrigation set-up in the shop that's not connected to anything right now. And there were L-shaped rust marks on the floor, in a pattern under the light fixtures, right about where each foot of the shelving units would sit. Each light fixture has a socket for an add-on light. Probably had the units stacked two-high, not six-high like they are now. Sarge, the place was clean—too clean. I bet he'd just moved the plants into the house."

Macgregor grunted. "Alleged plants."

Angie shrugged. "I'm convinced. Of course, he could be growing his very own purely organic vegetables."

"Supplementing his income through the weekly farmers' market," grinned Macgregor. "Where's he employed?"

Angie wrinkled her brow. "Right now, he's not. He worked at the Clanton Mine until it closed, got a good severance package and some other benefits, employment insurance is due to run out in a couple of months. Might be why he's diversifying."

"Okay. Angie, you're following up on the bikes in this guy's shop. Get me some connection here, something to put Franco together with the stolen Harleys. Harland, get a team out with the dog to cover the walking route between Jugs and the residence. Let the wife know the media's on it. And let me know what the lab says about the blood. Actually, keep me posted about anything else that comes in."

ELLEN LOOKED UP from the flower bed. The police cruiser was pulling to a stop, and she was somewhat relieved to see that Constable Harland had come alone. She stood, peeling off her gloves. "Monte, don't knock the man over."

"Hello, Monte." He pulled off his sunglasses. "Good afternoon, Mrs. Hoskins."

So formal. Perhaps he had to keep his distance until he was sure he wouldn't have to arrest her. "Would it be a problem to call me Ellen?"

"Sure. I mean, no—it wouldn't be a problem. I'm John."

She smiled. "John. Any news?"

"Some. Nothing concrete." He opened his notebook.

"Would you like to come in?" She really didn't want to do this in the front yard.

Do what, spend time chatting with a charming man? Or find out she was a suspect?

"It is rather warm out. You're back-door people, aren't you?" Monte trotted at his heels. "My folks are, too. My mother claims front doors are just for salesmen and bad news."

Ellen smiled, opening the door. "Monte, wait your turn! I'm sorry. He usually has better manners."

John laughed, following the dog into the back porch. "No problem. Border collie?"

"Mostly. He was a stray, so I'm not sure. Lemonade?"

"Please." He was standing in the doorway between the kitchen and the porch, rubbing Monte's ears. "We had a border collie on the farm. You see lots of them in rural areas, but not so many in town. Probably because they like to work. I'll bet he's pretty active?"

Ellen put out two glasses and pulled a pitcher from the fridge. "Oh, yes. We put in plenty of w-a-l-k time. And I've recently discovered that the neighbor's boy has been coming over and playing with Monte when he thinks nobody's around." She put half a dozen cookies on a plate.

"Why does he wait until nobody's around?"

"Afraid of Stan." She put the cookies on the table and sat down. "Jason's a nice kid; been in the neighborhood a few months. His father died in a car accident and his mother has been working two jobs. Shame, really. You'd think there would be some insurance or something, with them having had a child and all."

Harland settled into the chair nearest the door, one hand still resting on Monte's head. He reached for a cookie with the other. "Sometimes it gets tangled up in red tape for a while." He bit into the cookie. "Mmm. These are just the best. Also, sometimes folks anticipate an insurance payment and get themselves in over their heads before the payout. Then they're in trouble if the payout's not what they expected, or some other debt crops up that they weren't aware of."

Unexpected debts? Ellen hadn't thought about this. What if Stan had borrowed money she didn't know about?

"Ellen, you sure you're alright until we find your husband?" He looked at her. "I'm sorry, that's really none of my business."

Ellen swallowed. "Stan was actually a financial liability, so finances shouldn't be an issue. It hadn't occurred to me that he might have gone into debt, though. But I would know, wouldn't I? I would have to co-sign."

"Not necessarily. Did Stan have a good credit rating?"

Ellen shook her head. "Bad. I took over the finances after we lost the car."

"So he probably couldn't have gotten anything much in the way of a loan without you knowing about it. Don't worry. I'm sure it will be fine."

Don't worry, li'l lady. Ellen smiled. "Have you found anything new?"

Harland nodded. "I'm afraid so. It doesn't look good, Ellen. I spoke again with Ms. Simms this morning. She was able to corroborate the statement we got from the witness yesterday."

Ellen reached for her lemonade, but when she realized her hand was shaking she folded her hands in her lap instead. "Clarissa was here this morning. She told me about… about Franco. And that Stan might have fallen into the ditching. Or jumped. She wasn't sure it was him."

"Our other witness *was* sure that Stan was there."

"Oh." Ellen clasped her hands together, hard. "Did the other witness see… where Stan went?"

Harland shook his head. "I'm sorry. He waited for a little while after Clarissa was gone, then he left the park."

"He didn't… didn't think to call the police?"

"No."

"Why not?"

"I can't say. Ellen, it's still possible that Stan is alive, just dazed. And we're not entirely sure we can rely on our witness. It could still turn out Stan wasn't at the park at all. Search and Rescue is helping a crew of our people; they're scouring the area between Jugs and your house. And we've started a media campaign. I'm sorry, there really is no other way."

Ellen swallowed. "I understand. It just seems so… so big, now. Before, he was just late coming home."

"I'll need a couple of personal articles of Stan's. Clothing that hasn't been washed since he wore it."

Ellen looked at him. "Are they bringing in dogs?"

Harland nodded. "They start this afternoon."

She smiled. "I love the idea of police dogs." She glanced at Monte, who had settled on the floor, mostly in the porch, but with his head and forepaws near the back leg of Harland's chair. "Could I… oh, I guess that wouldn't seem…"

"I don't think you should be in the area. It might confuse the dogs, plus the media will be there. But they should be searching right to your door, so you might see them."

Right to her door.

Ellen looked across the table at Harland, who smiled and reached for another cookie. Did that mean she was a suspect? *Don't be silly,* she thought. *If I were a suspect, he would have brought Constable Wilson with him.*

Wouldn't he have?

Maybe this cozy chat was a front. A way to get her guard down.

She felt Harland eyes on her. "Are you alright, Ellen?

"Oh. Yes, of course. I'll get you some things. Of Stan's. Clothing? You mean like a sweatshirt or something?"

"That would be fine."

"Excuse me a moment."

In the bedroom, Ellen leaned against the dresser. "Get hold of yourself," she said under her breath.

Something of Stan's. She looked around the room she had shared with him for fourteen years. Fourteen years less a day. Or rather, less a night. Every night for fourteen years, lying in that bed with a man she didn't love. Worse, a man that she loathed. Yes, loathed. Loathed when he reached for her, knowing she could be anyone, anyone with breasts and a— Loathed when he touched her, took her with his harsh, clumsy urgency. Loathed the routine, mechanical mating, untempered by any tenderness, ungentled by any love. *Loathed* him. Loathed him utterly and—

The sudden ripping noise startled Ellen, and she looked down with surprise. Her hands were clenched around Stan's navy sweatshirt, their distended veins almost the color of the faded fabric. A hole had appeared beneath one sleeve; the seam had given way under her furious twisting. She flung the shirt from her and covered her face with her hands. A sharp bark from Monte brought her to her senses.

"I think you have company," called Harland.

The back gate thumped. Picking up the shirt, she returned to the kitchen. There was a quick knock, then the door opened and Clarissa popped her head in.

"Just me. Oh, sorry, Constable Harland. I didn't realize I was interrupting." She looked at Ellen. "News?"

Ellen shook her head. "Nothing. John was just picking up some things of Stan's. They're starting a search."

"Oh." Clarissa hooked her purse on the doorknob, her eyes searching Ellen's face. "I suppose it's time. You okay?"

"Yes. I just… I just need a bag. For this shirt. And another one for… I'll have to get something else, too. You said a couple of things. Two things."

Harland had stood when Clarissa entered, and he smiled at Ellen. "Two would be fine. Thank you, Ellen."

Ellen returned to the bedroom, opened the closet and pulled out a pair of slippers. She took a deep breath and headed back to the kitchen.

"… out of the news," Clarissa hissed, glaring at Harland.

Ellen smiled. "Clarissa, I'm okay. Really. It's not John's fault. This has to be done."

"I suppose so." Clarissa shrugged. "But you'll probably get every crack-pot and weirdo in town calling you now. I came over to unplug your phone."

"Unplug it? Why?"

"I just told you."

"But then *you* can't call me."

Clarissa smiled. "Ellie, how often do I bother to announce my arrival?" She turned to Harland. "And you, Constable John Harland. You don't always call ahead, do you? You know where—"

The phone rang. "Excuse me." Ellen passed Harland the clothing and picked up the phone. "Hello?"

"Mrs. Hoskins?" the voice on the line rasped.

"Yes, this is Mrs. Hos—"

"You're wasting my tax dollars to find that scumbag husband of yours. You want the sonofabitch back, you should be out there lookin' for him. Take my hard-earned tax money to pay our cops to look for that jerk? Cops otta be out solving crimes, keeping people safe from…"

Ellen wasn't aware that Harland had crossed the room until he took the phone from her trembling grasp. He held it to his ear for a second, then hung up, reached down, and unplugged it from the wall. Clarissa already had her arms around Ellen when he stood up, and he left them to go from room to room. "I found another phone in the office," he said. "Any others?"

Clarissa shook her head.

"Ellen, Ms. Simms is right. Leave your phones unplugged."

Ellen turned and looked up at him. "Don't be silly. That was… that was just one person. What if you need to get hold of me?"

"I'll drive over."

"What if you can't?"

Clarissa pointed to her bag. "I've got my cell. Ellie, I'm staying with you tonight." She held up her hand. "No arguments. The boys have gone camping with Dave's parents, and I'm off work. You'll feed me supper, and I'll sleep on the couch." She turned to Harland. "Get out your notebook, Constable John Harland, and write this number down."

Ellen shook Clarissa's arm. "Clarissa, calm down. You don't need to stay here. This is silly."

Harland flipped open his notebook. "Ellen, why not let Ms. Simms take care of you tonight."

"Thank you, Constable Harland. And drop the Ms. Simms." She smiled at him sweetly. "It's Clarissa."

SIXTEEN

CLARISSA STACKED THE SUPPER DISHES in the sink, then turned to Ellen. "Let's leave these and take Monte for a walk. I don't like the look of that sky."

Ellen set her teacup down and leaned over to look out the window. "Looks like a good storm brewing. You want to borrow a jacket?"

"We'll swing by my place and grab one." Clarissa slid her feet into her sandals and reached for Monte's leash.

Ellen pulled on a light jacket and her walking shoes. "You leaving your bag here?"

"Sure. Grab my phone though. Got room for it in your pocket?"

Ellen nodded. Monte squirmed through the door as soon as it opened, and he and Clarissa headed for the gate while Ellen locked the door.

The neighbors' door banged shut. "Hey, Ellen!"

She turned. "Hi, Jason. How's it going?"

"Good. I mean, good for me. Mom's doing better, too. She picked me up from school today, and we went out for supper to celebrate. She can quit one of her jobs now. The guy riding in the taxi in my dad's accident was trying to sue her, but he never showed up for court today. So the judge threw it out."

Ellen crossed to the fence. "Oh, Jason. That is good news. Your mom must be very relieved."

"Yeah. Wish she'd told me about it sooner. No wonder she was so totally stressed out. Anyways, now there's no lawyer bills so she's just keeping the job she likes. No more fast food."

Ellen smiled. "That's wonderful. Jason, this is my friend Clarissa Simms."

Jason held his hand out over the fence. "Nice to meet you, Miss Simms."

"Clarissa. Nice to meet you, too, Jason. Ellen tells me you've been helping her keep Monte entertained."

"Yeah. He's a great dog. Arn'tcha, boy." He reached in his pocket for a kibble. "Sorry. Nothing there." He looked up at Ellen. "Mr. Hoskins is still missing?"

Ellen nodded. "We need to walk Monte before the storm sets in. Tell your mom I'm very happy for her good news."

"I will." There was a distant rumble, and Jason sprinted toward the house. "Nice meeting you, Clarice," he called over his shoulder.

"Clarissa. Likewise, Jason," called Clarissa. "Nice

kid," she added as they headed through Ellen's gate. "His dad was killed in an accident with a taxi?"

"Apparently. And the passenger... oh, lord. Clarissa." Ellen clutched her friend's arm.

"Mmm. You figure Stan's neck brace was all about suing that family?"

"He didn't..." Of course, he wouldn't have told her. "Imagine, them moving right next door."

"Too weird," said Clarissa. "At least they're off the hook now. Even if Stan shows up again, the judge has thrown it out. And if Stan tries to make it an issue again, I'm prepared to let Jason's mom know just how much that stupid neck brace was really used."

"Want me to take the leash?"

"No, I hardly ever get to look after Monte. Think you'll travel a bit more now?"

"We'll see." Monte led them across York, then turned right. "Didn't you want to go straight to your place?"

"We can come back that way," said Clarissa. "Monte's already chosen the route. You go this way every day?"

"Most," said Ellen. "Once in a while we shake things up. Oh, hello, Mr. Shakespeare."

The man sitting on the porch raised his hand. "Ah, fair Desdemona. 'Tis Will, I beseech thee." He stood, then he stiffened and paled. "What are you doing with that lady?"

"Will, this is my good friend Clarissa."

"Friend? Friend, you say?" Hesitantly, he approached. Then he smiled. "Ah, I see. 'Tis Emilia. A thousand pardons, good lady. I mistook thee for someone else." He bowed low.

Clarissa looked bewildered for a moment, then smiled. "Nice to meet you."

"Ah, the pleasure is all mine." He bowed low again, and spoke quietly. "Hast thou returned to Desdemona that which is hers?"

"Pardon?"

"The napkin! The napkin, good woman!"

"Napkin?"

"Thou didst have thy ladies napkin. Didst thou give it her?"

"Give it her? I'm sorry, I'm not sure what you mean."

He shook his head impatiently and turned to Ellen. "A thousand pardons, my lady. I wouldst have a word with thy companion."

Ellen smiled. "Sure. I'll just admire your beautiful yard." She took a few steps farther along the sidewalk, shrugging at Clarissa.

"Good lady," he said in a stage whisper that carried to where Ellen stood, clutching Clarissa's sleeve, "prithee listen! Should thee find thy ladies napkin, that most prized of her possessions, *give it not to thy husband.*"

Clarissa took a step back. "My husband?"

"Aye! Give it not to Iago. Return it at once to thy mistress."

"My mistress!"

"Aye. Thy mistress, Desdemona." He tilted his head toward Ellen.

"Oh. If I find her napkin, give it to her." She looked at Ellen, who shrugged and smiled. "Not to my husband."

He sagged with relief. "Aye. Give it not to Iago, else shalt there be wrought such scenes of horror, and of misery—" A crash of thunder interrupted him, and he looked to the sky. "A tempest," he said.

"Tempest?"

"Aye." A gust of wind whipped through the yard, rattling the branches of the rose bush and sending a shower of petals swirling through the air. Another crash of thunder, and Monte put his head back and howled. "A plague upon this howling! They are louder than the weather, or our office." Speare turned his back on Clarissa. "Yet again? What do you here?" Shaking his fist in the air, he strode toward the back yard. "Shall we give o'er and drown? Have you a mind to sink?"

Clarissa pulled a pack of cigarettes from her pocket and

turned to Ellen, who was calming Monte. "What the hell was that all about?" She fumbled for her lighter.

Ellen laughed. "He's harmless. He just doesn't live in the real world."

"So I gathered." Clarissa walked with her back to the wind, struggling to light her cigarette. "But what was he going on about? That thing about the napkin?"

They crossed Government and turned right, hurrying toward Clarissa's.

"It's from the play Othello. He thinks I'm Desdemona, Othello's wife, and I am about to be killed in a jealous rage."

"Great. So who's Emilia? Some kind of lady-in-waiting?"

"More of a companion. She's married to Iago. Othello is some kind of general or something, in the army. He just got a promotion, and Iago is all bent out of shape because he thinks the promotion should have gone to him. So he's quite jealous of Othello."

"So he kills Des-… Desda-… Othello's wife?"

"Oh, no." Ellen turned onto the path through the park. "He's much too nefarious for that. Instead, he tries to make Othello think that Desdemona is having an affair with one of the men."

"Is she?"

"Of course not. Othello doesn't believe him. But then Iago sees that his own wife—Desdemona's friend, Emilia— has found the napkin."

"What napkin?" Clarissa scooted through the opening into the alley.

"Desdemona's napkin. It's some kind of handkerchief, and for some reason it's one of her favorite treasures. In the play, she always carries it around with her. Kind of goofy, but Shakespeare doesn't always make sense."

"Ah, so Emilia has the napkin, and she gives it to Iago. Her husband. The arch-enemy of Desdemona's husband, Othello."

"Right. And he uses it... I forget exactly what he does with it, but Othello finally believes Desdemona is stepping out on him."

"Twisted." Clarissa stopped in the entry to her back gate, reaching to extinguish her cigarette. "Damn. Ellen, why the hell would anyone steal my ashtray?" She dropped the butt on the path, ground it out with her sandal, and kicked the butt back out into the alley.

"Somebody probably felt sorry for it and turned it into a nice, respectable planter."

Clarissa snorted. "Well, dammit, it wasn't theirs to take. First thing I've had stolen from the yard since I moved here. I gotta get a dog. So, back to Othello. Don't tell me, let me guess. Everybody dies."

Ellen smiled. "Well, it is one of his tragedies." She took Monte's leash while Clarissa unlocked the door. "There's a terrific version of it on video at the library. Kenneth Brannagh and Laurence Fishburne. We should get it."

Clarissa ran into the house. As she reappeared with her jacket, hard drops of rain pelted down. "Perfect! Pajama party at Ellie's. Let's take the car, then. Monte, want to go on a field trip? Car?" She opened the front gate.

Another crash of thunder, and Monte bolted for the car, shivering while he waited for Clarissa to unlock the door.

They piled in after him, laughing. Clarissa started the engine and cranked the wipers to full speed. "Wow! Look at this rain. Good night to curl up with videos and popcorn. Hey, let's get *How Stella Got Her Groove Back,* and *Shirley Valentine.*"

"Shirley who?"

"Oh, girl, where you been?" Clarissa backed into the street. "We on a mission, Monte. We gotta get yo' momma some groove. It ain't lost. She jes' ain't grown none yet!"

ELLEN CLOSED THE BACK DOOR softly and hung up Monte's leash. His tail thumped against the door. Clarissa dragged herself into the kitchen, clutching her ears. "Oh, my god, make it stop. How much did I drink?"

Ellen smiled. "Good morning, sleeping beauty. Got a bad head?"

Clarissa groaned and sank into a chair. "I think my cell phone was ringing. Did you get it?"

Ellen shook her head. "I was over at Jason's, having tea with his very nice, very relieved mother. Oh, and Stan had nothing whatsoever to do with her husband's accident. We've got to quit seeing bogeymen everywhere."

Clarissa was entirely unresponsive.

Ellen crossed her arms. "Do you know what time it is, young lady?"

"No."

"It's eleven o'clock."

"Oh." Clarissa's eyes widened. "What day? Ellie, tell me it's not Saturday!"

"Friday. You don't work until four. Plenty of time for a shower, and a nice brunch."

"No food. No food. Just…" Clarissa clacked her tongue against the roof of her mouth. "Just water."

"Coming right up, my lady." Ellen headed for the cupboard.

"My lady. Right. Who am I again?"

"Well, according to Mr. Shakespeare, you're Emilia."

"Right. And you're Desdemona."

Ellen set a glass of water in front of Clarissa, who still had her head in her hands on the tabletop. "But according to you, it's the other way around."

Clarissa sat up, wincing, and reached for the water. "Thanks. Yeah. You're more giving, and I'm more self-absorbed." She swallowed. "What did you think of Shirley Valentine?"

Ellen smiled. "Loved it. Missed a bit of the dialogue on account of your snoring, but otherwise…"

Clarissa glared at her, then winced. "I don't snore."

Ellen shrugged. "Suit yourself."

Clarissa took another sip, then pulled herself upright and staggered back to the couch. "Aaargh, my head. So, are you ready to head to the Mediterranean?"

Ellen shook her head. "It was a great movie, but I can't see myself doing it."

Clarissa scowled. "Doing what? Ditching your husband or heading out on a well-earned vacation?"

Ellen sighed and settled into the armchair. "Neither."

Clarissa looked at the end table. She pulled a sock off her foot, set it on the hardwood table, and put her glass on top of it. "Why not?"

Ellen pulled open a drawer and took out a coaster, dumping the sock on the floor. "I'm not Shirley."

"You could be. Too bad they didn't have Stella." Clarissa clutched her head.

"Why, you think I'd be a good Stella? Get my groove back, whatever the heck that means?"

"We'll get her on pay per view at my place next time, and you can decide."

In the street, a car pulled to a stop; a door thumped. Monte gave a low woof as footsteps approached.

Clarissa moaned, pulled herself to her feet and headed for the bathroom. The footsteps gained the porch. Monte barked, and there was a firm knock at the front door.

"Thanks, Monte," said Ellen, opening the door. Her smile froze. Behind John Harland stood Constable Angie Wilson.

"Good morning, Mrs. Hoskins," he said.

Mrs. Hoskins. Front door. Salesmen and...

"Bad news," she said softly. "Good morning, Constable Harland. Constable Wilson. Please, come in."

She picked up the blanket and pillow from the couch, and headed for the bedroom. "Please, have a seat."

Ellen dumped the blanket on her bed, took a deep breath, and returned to the living room. Constable Wilson had settled into the armchair. Constable Harland stood awkwardly, looking utterly miserable.

"What's happened?"

"Please, Mrs. Hoskins, have a seat. Is Ms. Simms still here?"

Ellen felt rooted to the ground. "She's in the bathroom."

Constable Harland took her elbow, leading her gently to the couch.

Constable Wilson looked at Ellen. "I'm sorry, Mrs. Hoskins. This morning, a city work crew found Mr. Hoskins. I'm afraid he's dead."

ELLEN SAGGED BACK against the couch. Harland glanced at Angie, who looked back at him without expression. He turned back to Ellen. She was leaning forward now, elbows on her knees, her face buried in her hands.

Angie leaned forward, too. "I'm afraid there's more, Mrs. Hoskins." She waited until Ellen tilted her head up to look at her. "We found the weapon beside Ms. Simms' back gate."

The bathroom door opened, and Clarissa came down the hall. She stopped when she saw Constable Wilson, glanced up at Harland, then down at Ellen. She hurried over to the couch, settling protectively next to Ellen. "What's happened?"

Ellen clung to her. "They've found Stan."

"Where the hell has he been?" She looked up at him.

Harland searched for the right words. "He's been... I'm afraid he's dead."

Clarissa's eyes widened. "Oh, my god. How?"

Angie was matter-of-fact. "He was found in the storm drain on Government Street. We won't know until the autopsy, but it looks like he died from one or more blows to the head."

"Blows..."

"That's right. Ms. Simms, we'd like to take you downtown for questioning."

Ellen grabbed Clarissa's arm. "Why? She didn't do it. What... what weapon did you find?"

Clarissa looked up at Harland. "Weapon?"

Harland forced his voice to sound businesslike. "Ms. Simms, there were traces of Stan's blood on your ashtray."

"My what?"

"Your ashtray. The old-fashioned floor-standing one beside your gate. The dogs lead us to it yesterday."

Clarissa stood up, glaring at him. "That ashtray has been missing for days."

"It was in your yard yesterday afternoon."

Angie got to her feet. "Ms. Simms, you say the ashtray has been missing for days. Since when?"

"I don't remember. A week? It's not like it's something I use every day."

"Can anyone confirm this?"

"*Confirm* it? Of course not. Somebody *boosted* my *ashtray*. What do you mean, *confirm* it?"

Angie looked at her. "Ms. Simms, you admit to being at Knight's Park on the night Mr. Hoskins disappeared. The probable murder weapon was found in your yard. We would like you to come downtown with us, now, for questioning."

Clarissa raised her chin. "Fine." She glared at Harland. "Shall I call my lawyer?"

Harland shook his head. "It's just routine. Nobody's saying you..."

Angie interrupted. "Of course you can, Ms. Simms. Under the circumstances, it might be a good idea."

Ellen leaped to her feet. "No. No. It wasn't Clarissa. She didn't do it. She didn't have anything to do with it." She stepped forward, shielding Clarissa. "It was me. I did it. I killed Stan."

SEVENTEEN

CLARISSA MOVED AROUND ELLEN. "Don't listen to her," she said. "She's just being overprotective." She turned to face Ellen. "Look, Ellie. I know what you're doing. But you don't need to. I didn't have anything to do with this. Just let me go downtown with them, and we'll sort it out. You'll see."

"You don't understand, Clarissa. I did it. I b—"

Clarissa clamped her hand over Ellen's mouth. "You did not." Still holding her hand firmly in place, she turned to Harland. "If you'll wait in the car, officer, I'll just get my bag and join you in a moment."

Harland nodded, relieved, but Angie intervened. "You'll both need to come down to the station. Constable Harland, it's time to go."

Harland swallowed. "Mrs. Hoskins, we'll take your statement at the station." He turned to Clarissa. "Ms. Simms, has the dog been walked?"

She nodded, glaring at him, and his guts twisted harder.

"Alright." He turned to Ellen. "Mrs. Hoskins, would you like Monte to be left indoors or out?"

Clarissa looked at Ellen, and slowly removed her hand.

Ellen spoke quietly. "Out, please. Clarissa, can you come after work and take him for a walk, then put him in for the night?"

Clarissa stared at her. "Ellen, stop it. You'll be home in an hour. And if you're not, I'll be damned if I'll be going to work."

"But I—"

Clarissa clamped her hand back over Ellen's mouth. "Stop it," she hissed. She looked pleadingly at Harland. "Please. She's just taking care of me." She turned back to Ellen. "Ellie, stop. Now. There's no need for this. I didn't do anything wrong."

Harland turned to Angie. "Is this really necessary?"

Angie's eyebrows bounced.

He clenched his jaw. Of course it was necessary. What

was he, and idiot? Ellen had just admitted to killing her husband, and here he was suggesting that she didn't really have to go down to the station. He turned to Clarissa. Any moment she might take her hand off Ellen's mouth and whack it across his face. He cleared his throat. "Let's go. I'm sure this will be cleared up in no time."

He ignored Angie's pity, Clarissa's fury. Tried to ignore Ellen's stoic calm.

Clarissa gave Ellen another glare of warning before slowly removing her hand. She reached for her bag. "Get your keys and our shoes, Ellen," she said.

Ellen went to the porch, picked up her shoes, Clarissa's sandals, her keys. Bending, she patted Monte. "Go outside, boy." She opened the back door and let him out, then locked it closed.

Resisting an urge to put his arm around her shoulder, Harland crossed to the front door and opened it. "Ladies." Too late, he saw the television crew on the street. The cameraman was frantically pulling his equipment from the van. Monte barked furiously from the side yard. "Ellen, give me your keys. Angie, get them in the car. Quick."

They hurried down the steps, Clarissa holding Ellen protectively, trying to shield her face. On the sidewalk, a reporter from the daily paper snapped photos. Behind her, a television camera was pointed in their direction and Clarissa spread one hand over Ellen's face as she pushed her into the car.

Harland locked the house. "Stay, Monte." He closed the front gate, then wrenched open the passenger door.

A reporter stepped forward. "Officer, can you tell us if these women are suspects?"

"No comment." Harland closed his door, and Angie pulled away from the curb.

He turned to the back seat. "You okay?"

"Just dandy," said Clarissa.

He turned to Angie. "You radio it in?"

"Nope. Go ahead."

Harland pressed the button on the mike and reported their whereabouts to the office, aware of Angie's sidelong looks.

She clearly figured he'd lost it.

But hell's bells, what was she thinking? Ellen's claim was obviously just what Clarissa said it was: a cooked-up story to protect her friend. Couldn't Angie see that Ellen wouldn't hurt a fly? He hung up the mike, and they rode to the station in silence.

ANGIE PUSHED THE REMOTE OPENER, pulled into the secure parking area, waited until the door swung closed behind them. "Let's go."

Harland stood by while the women climbed out of the back seat. Inside the station, he escorted them into a room with a table and four chairs.

"Wait here," said Angie. "Harland, you come with me." Stepping into the hall, she pulled the door closed. "John, you can't question either of these women."

He looked at her. "Why not?"

She drew herself up to full height. "Because, John, you are involved."

"What the hell do you mean, involved?"

"You know exactly what I mean. Anything you get out of Mrs. Hoskins shouldn't be allowed in a court of law. And as for Ms. Simms, she hasn't given you a straight line yet."

Macgregor crossed the room. "What's this about?"

Angie turned to him. "Sarge, we went to pick up the Simms woman. She was at the Hoskins' residence."

"And?"

"And she said she had nothing to do with it. We wanted her to come downtown anyway. At that point, Mrs. Hoskins confessed."

Macgregor snorted. "The widow confessed?"

Harland could feel his face heating. "Angie, you know damn well that was no confession. Sarge, Mrs. Hoskins was just protecting Ms. Simms. Obviously, she thinks her friend might have had something to do with it."

"And did she?"

"Who?"

"Simms! Did she have anything to do with it?"

"No! At least, I doubt it. Just because she didn't volunteer every little thing she knew…"

Angie held up her hand. "She didn't volunteer *anything.*"

Harland turned to her. "Angie, that's not fair. You've said yourself, some people you have to pry it out of them with a crowbar. Hell. That doesn't mean she's guilty."

Macgregor turned to him. "Harland, Angie's right. I want her to question Simms. You question the wife."

"But he—"

Macgregor shook his head. "Look, we're short staffed here with people out on flood control, and we've got the makings of a media circus outside. Get on with it. And let me know when you're done."

HARLAND SIGHED, RUNNING HIS HANDS over his face. Damn. He shoved the stack of files aside. Damn it all to hell. From across the room, he could feel Angie's eyes on him. He ignored her.

What the hell did all this mean?

Ellen had sat across the desk from him, calmly giving her statement.

No, she didn't want a lawyer. Yes, she had killed her husband. No, she hadn't struck him. She'd found him at the bottom of the ditch, more dead than alive. No, she hadn't gone for help. Because she wanted him dead. That's why she was out looking for him. That's why she brought a shovel.

Brought a *shovel?* Harland' mouth had gone dry. Why?

Because it was their anniversary, and she was tired of the whole charade.

But a *shovel?* It made no sense.

No, she supposed it didn't.

Why not divorce?

Divorce? Ellen's mouth had twisted slightly. Although Stan had no real use for her, he did consider her to be his. His property. He'd told her, and she believed him, that if she left he would find her and kill her. But not right away. Not until he got through with Monte. He had plans for Monte, and he wanted her—Ellen's eyes had welled up, and she had fought for control—and he wanted her to watch. No, Constable Harland. Divorce was not an option. So she had gone out, in the middle of the night, with a shovel.

Why a shovel?

Ellen had shrugged. It seemed like a good idea at the time.

What was she planning to do, bonk him on the head with it?

No answer.

Did she honestly think she would use it?

Another silent shrug.

So when she found Stan more dead than alive at the bottom of the ditch in front of Knight's Park, what did she do?

She buried him.

Buried him? *Alive?*

Well, no. Sometime after she had started digging the hole, he had gurgled his last breath. He'd never regained consciousness.

So why had she *said* that she killed him?

Because if she had gotten help, he might have lived.

And why hadn't she gotten help?

Again the shrug. Because she'd had enough. She wanted him dead. Besides, if help came, how would she explain the shovel?

Harland's hand shook as he flipped the page of his notebook. So, if Stan hadn't died, would she have buried him anyway?

Silence. Then, ever so quietly, "Who knows?"

He stared down at his notebook.

The silence stretched on, Ellen staring vacantly out the window beside his desk, until a sudden downpour pelted the pavement outside.

"It was the rain," she said, closing her eyes, rocking gently. Then Angie came to escort her to the cells.

HARLAND LOOKED UP, STARTLED. Angie had perched on his desk.

He ignored her, and looked out the window. The rain had slowed to a drizzle. He really should start typing up Ellen's statement.

Angie put a cup of coffee on the desk, and he realized she had been gone and returned. He glanced at the clock. Four-fifteen. He looked at the still-blank form.

Angie was saying something. What? He couldn't focus.

"John." Angie leaned over, her face in front of his. "Look at me."

He stared at her, tried to concentrate on what she was saying. The city works crew had dug Stan out when their brand-new storm drain system backed up. The corpse had been lodged in the pipe, partway between Knight's Park and Warrick. The water had backed into the street and over the sidewalk, creating a stream that washed into every driveway on the block as it chased its furious way toward the next intersection.

Hardest hit was Franklin Anderson's house, where the water had found an easy entry through in the depression at his front gate. From there the newborn creek ran along Franco's front path and careened around the house, following the path along the side then down the stairs, pouring through the dog door and into his walk-in basement. Work crews had broken into the basement to rescue the howling dog and found forty mature pot plants, twenty-nine thousand in cash, and two of the stolen Harleys.

Harland tried to make sense—

Lodged in the pipe.

His eyes widened.

Lodged. In the pipe.

He leapt to his feet. "Angie, you're an angel. I love you."

She grinned. "Yeah, yeah. I know."

"Where's Ellen?"

"In lock-up."

Harland scowled. "And Clarissa?"

"Released." Angie sighed. "You know, I think you were right about her. Probably about both of them."

"You don't think they had anything to do with it?"

"I doubt it." Angie shook her head. "Here's what I figure. I think Clarissa would have liked to kill Stan on Ellen's behalf, but she didn't do it. I think Ellen knew Clarissa wanted to do it, and because of the way things went down, she thought maybe she had. So. Questioning went okay?"

Harland could feel his face flushing, and he was relieved when Angie turned to pick up the files. "I told Sarge you'd be in to report after you'd had your coffee," she said. "Drink up; won't stay hot forever."

Harland reached for his mug as she held the files toward him. They bumped, and the cup tilted, sloshing over his open notebook.

"Damn." Standing, Harland grabbed the notebook and tore off the wet pages and held them, dripping, over the desk.

"I'll get some paper towel," said Angie, heading for the lunch room. As she passed her desk, her phone rang. She turned and signaled to Harland, picking up the phone.

He dropped the sodden paper on his desk top and headed for the lunch room, grabbing a handful of napkins.

Misha was waiting for him at his desk. "John, the sergeant wants you in his office five minutes ago." She took the napkins from him. "I'll mop that up. Get Angie off the phone if you can, and get in there before he explodes."

"Thanks, Misha. I owe you." Angie was hanging up,

and Harland tilted his head toward Macgregor's office. "We've been summoned."

Macgregor looked up from his desk. "Well, it's about time," he growled. "Fill me in."

EIGHTEEN

ELLEN SAT ON THE EDGE of the vinyl mattress. The cell was small, with metal beds firmly attached to two of the concrete-block walls, and a stainless steel sink and toilet combination mounted against the third. The fourth wall was bars. One section could slide open sideways but was now closed, and firmly locked.

At the cell block desk, Constable Wilson had asked her to empty her pockets, then "frisked" her while the guard recorded her belongings in duplicate on an intake form: keys, watch, wallet. Cash went into a sealed envelope: two five-dollar bills. Each item went into a small cloth sack.

"Sign here, please." The guard's voice was neutral, her face blank as she held out the pen. Ellen signed beside the X. "I'll need your shoes."

Ellen had handed them to the guard, who took them and the sack to a small room that contained a small block of lockers.

"Four," said the guard.

Constable Wilson noted the locker number on the intake sheet, then turned to leave. "Give her a couple of blankets, Paula."

The guard had stopped on her way out of the room and picked up a gray wool blanket from the stack by the door. She tore open a thin film of plastic dry-cleaning wrap and pulled out another blanket. "Follow me." She pushed open a thick metal door with a small, eye-level window covered by a sliding metal plate, and Ellen followed her through into a room that was divided in half by the wall of bars.

Paula had stopped at the opening in the bars, handed Ellen the blankets, and waited for her to step through before sliding the door shut. The bars clanged, reverberating. She'd pulled a chain from her hip, inserted the key into the lock, turned it, tugged at the bars, nodded, and swung the heavy metal door part-way closed behind her as she left.

Behind that door, mounted from the ceiling, was a video camera.

Was someone watching? Ellen wondered how long she had been sitting; her feet were cold, and she looked down at the folded blankets on the bed beside her. They were coarse and scratchy, but they were clean. She looked at the mattress. What was that all over one side of it? She leaned closer. Just a stain. The heavy vinyl covering smelled clean. She set one of the blankets at the end of the bed like a pillow, and used the other to cover herself.

There was no sound from the guard's desk, from outside. It was cold in the cell, and quiet as death.

Quiet as death.

Death was quiet. Dying wasn't. Not in Stan's case, anyway. He had screamed. Like an animal, Clarissa said. Ellen closed her eyes, shuddering. Of course, that wasn't his death. That was from the assault. He had obviously died some time later, in the ditch.

Had the blows killed him, or had the fall finished him off? His head was at an odd angle when Ellen found him, but he was still alive. It was his loud breathing that had attracted her attention as she marched down the sidewalk, heading toward the path through Knight's Park, her mind a curious combination of calm and turmoil.

Why had she not seen the witness, the one the police thought might not be reliable? Who had she ever seen out at that late hour, on her nocturnal walks with Monte? A couple of times she'd seen a teenager or two walking home (good thing they were on foot, in the shape they were in) and she'd wondered if their parents knew they were three sheets to the wind in a deserted park, at that hour.

A few years ago she had started seeing a older woman asleep on the bench in the park. She hadn't been there for a few months, though, and Ellen hoped she had found a warmer place to spend the winter nights.

No, it had been a long time since she had seen anyone in the park up on her late-night walks. Even the streets were usually empty. Once in a blue moon, Mr. Shakespeare was pacing in his yard. Could it have been him, in the park that night? Not likely. She would have seen him. And he would have spoken to her, not hidden from her. Besides, the witness had seen Stan get hit. He had probably already left before Ellen even got to the park, and if it was Mr. Shakespeare she would have passed him on his way home.

Unless he didn't go straight home. Maybe he had followed Clarissa.

But why would he do that?

She pulled the blanket around her chin, trying to ignore the prickling.

The park, dark and unfriendly. A teen-aged boy, maybe eighteen, hunched against the darkness, feigning nonchalance as he stuffed his hands deeper into his denim jacket. No, his leather coat. That's why he was so hard to see. No, maybe he wore—Ellen frowned slightly. A picture of Robbie had sprung unbidden into her imagination. Not a teenager. They should all be safe at home.

The bag lady, then. There she was, sleeping on the bench, her arm protective across the cart containing her worldly goods, a breeze ruffling the scraggly bits of gray hair that poked out from under her knitted hat. Ellen shivered. No, not the bag lady, not that night. The poor woman would already be chilled before the rain started.

Mr. Shakespeare. He would enjoy being cast in the role.

Yes. There he is, standing under the trees.

No, he's slouched down on the bench, planning his latest production, awaiting inspiration from the woodland spirits. A noise from the north, and he turns to look; a man stumbles through the gate from the lane behind Government. The man has just cleared the fence when Clarissa lunges for him. *You've cheated on Ellen for the last time.*

Or maybe *You've embarrassed me in public for the last time.*

But maybe it isn't Clarissa. It's a big, nasty guy from Jugs. Clarissa's neighbor. Franco, she called him. *You've shot your mouth off once too often, Hoskins. Now you'll pay.*

No, he wouldn't say anything. He'd raise his weapon— Clarissa's ashtray?—and bring it down, hard, on Stan's foolish, unsuspecting head.

Ellen frowned. The attack wouldn't happen in the park. It would happen on the other side of the fence, in the lane.

Rewind.

Mr. Shakespeare is slumped peacefully on the bench, nodding off. Suddenly, he turns toward the lane. What was that dull thump? And that scream, like some wounded animal? He waits, tense, hardly breathing. Finally, a man stumbles through the opening. Is he hurt, or... wait. He has seen this guy before. He's coming home drunk from the bar again, and as for the scream—well, either it was his own scream of rage when he tripped over something, or it was an animal, screaming with pain as this brute kicked it out of his way.

He watches Stan stumble along the path. If the fool isn't careful, he's going to fall into the ditch. Mr. Shakespeare thinks he really ought to say something, warn him. *Ah, a thousand pardons, sir...*

Stan whirls toward Mr. Shakespeare.

No, wait. He's drunk.

He *turns,* clumsily, still stumbling toward the sidewalk, and sneers. *What're you lookin' at, you son-of-a—*

He stops in surprise, hangs mid-air for a second, cartoon-like, looks down at his feet, and then vanishes into the ditch.

Shakespeare is about to leap to his feet when another movement at the lane distracts him. Here comes a woman, with something big in her hand. What is she up to?

Oh, she's going to help Stan out of the ditch. How kind of her. The thing she's carrying is a pole about three feet long, with a foot-wide disk on either end. One disk has a handle. Ah! It's one of those old-fashioned ashtrays on a stand, like they use in hotels.

Should he acquire one for his plays?

Did they use them in Elizabethan England?

Probably not. Still, it would be a nice touch in the theatre lobby. If he allows smoking. He shouldn't. Filthy habit. But so many theatrical types smoke. After all, it's so… theatrical.

Okay, maybe outside.

The woman approaches the ditch. Shakespeare doesn't know whether or not to be disappointed: Stan's about to be rescued. Too bad, really. She'll let him grab one end and haul him out with the other. The woman kneels by the edge of the ditch. *Serves you right, you no-good, two-timing*—

Shakespeare's eyes widen in amazement as Clarissa raises the ashtray, bringing one end of it down, hard.

Ellen frowns again. Mr. Shakespeare didn't see anything like that. If he did, he would have reported it. Wouldn't he have? Of course he would have. He didn't trust Clarissa; until last night, he thought she was Lady Macbeth.

But then, she was just using Mr. Shakespeare for a witness. It could have been anyone. And anyone would have reported it, unless they were trying to protect Clarissa.

So who would protect Clarissa?

This is stupid, she thought; you have no idea what really happened.

Still, she couldn't shake off the fear that Clarissa had put some effort into finishing what Franco had started.

HARLAND LOOKED DOWN THE HALL to the lockup, but reluctantly turned in at the lunch room. He poured coffee into his cup, then swore under his breath. Coffee extract, probably brewed hours ago, thick and black as could be. He dumped it into the sink, rinsed the pot and filled it with fresh water, then tipped the filter basket into the garbage. He opened the cabinet. Damn. No filters. Hell's bells. Didn't anybody—

Angie appeared beside him. "Looking for these?"

"Yeah. Thanks." He tore open the package and put a filter into the basket, the rest into the cabinet.

"Get any sleep last night?" Angie spooned coffee into the filter.

"Some. What are you doing here on a Saturday?"

"Same as you." Angie slid the basket into place and flipped the switch. "I checked in at lock-up."

Harland wiped the counter, avoiding looking at her.

"She's fine. Paula says she's a model prisoner. They sat up half the night, talking."

Harland froze. "Talking?" He tried to make his voice casual. "About what?"

Angie rinsed out her mug. "Ellen ought to be a counselor. Paula claims she hasn't ever told a prisoner anything personal before, but she seems to have told Ellen her entire life story."

Harland smiled, relaxed a little. "Is Paula still here?"

"Just left." Angie turned and leaned against the sink. "Did you go straight home like I told you to?"

Harland didn't answer.

Angie shook her head. "How's her dog?"

"Good." Harland ignored Angie's frown of disapproval. "I saw Clarissa out walking him. I didn't stop in."

"I see."

Angie obviously had something to say. "What?"

"John, you've been in this line of work long enough to know the signs. Hoskins was thumping on his wife."

Harland's stomach churned.

"For the record, we haven't had this conversation."

"What?" He tried to focus.

"You know they'll see it as motive, so don't bring it up." Angie's jaw clenched. "Consider it one for Elaine."

Harland watched Angie turn toward the sink, realized

she'd clamped her hands around its rim as though to hold herself upright. He reached an arm across her shoulder.

"Don't. I'll be fine."

Harland gave her a quick squeeze and moved back to the table.

It had happened within his first few weeks on the job, but Angie still wouldn't talk about it. They'd been in the cruiser when the call came in. Just a routine call. Nothing special. Postie noticed the door open when he tried to put the mail through the slot, but no one was home. Angie recognized the address.

"That's my friend Elaine. Probably just didn't close the door properly." She picked up the mike. "We'll take this one." Setting the mike back, she'd smiled at Harland. "I haven't seen Elaine in ages. She's still in the honeymoon phase with her new guy; blows us girls off when we try to get her to come out with us."

The neighbors, an elderly couple, were already in the house, and one of them tried to keep Angie from entering, but she'd pushed past. They'd found Elaine in the bath, the water long since cold, a day-old bottle of prescription anti-depressants lying empty beside the toilet, her torso, arms and legs a tapestry of blues and greens and yellows anywhere her clothes would cover the bruises.

Elaine's husband arrived, his simpering "why would she do this" accompanied by a maudlin display of grief, the neighbors looking on with obvious disgust.

Harland had somehow sensed what Angie was going to do and pinned her arms to her sides in a bear hug, squeezing so she couldn't reach for the man, for her gun.

"Get him out of here," he'd said tersely to the officer who had just arrived, responding to the neighbor's 9-1-1 call.

"Son of a bitch." Angie'd crumpled against Harland as they took the husband to the car. "You should've let me—"

"Angie, the courts will—"

She'd laughed in his face. "God, you're naïve."

She was right. Elaine's husband would never see court, never be held accountable. He'd never acknowledge that he'd had a hand in the death of his wife.

"Coffee's ready." Angie brought the pot to the table, poured some into his mug. "I think you need to distance yourself from this, John. Or pass the case to someone else."

"I can handle it, Angie."

"Can you?"

The front door buzzer rang. "Guess I'll go get that."

Angie snorted. "Saved by the bell."

John stepped around the reception counter and opened the door to the street.

Clarissa turned to face him. "Oh. I just about left. I wasn't sure you'd be open today."

"We're not, usually." He held the door open for her. "Just happened to catch us in."

"I've brought some stuff for Ellen." She held up a plastic grocery bag. "Toothbrush, socks, underwear. And I want to see her."

"Of course." He held open the gate between the lobby and the office.

Angie appeared in the door of the lunch room. "Good morning, Ms. Simms."

Clarissa nodded stiffly. "Constable Wilson. I've come to see Ellen."

"She'll be pleased." Angie nodded at the bag. "You've brought her some things?"

Clarissa held it out. "I suppose you need to check it."

Angie took the bag. "Coffee?"

Clarissa shook her head firmly. Harland watched the women head toward the cells, then went into the lunch room and picked up his mug.

ELLEN RAN HER FINGERS through her hair. She was tempted to rinse her face, but the guard who had relieved Paula had not seemed very friendly, and she didn't want to ask him for paper towels. The cell had grown even colder overnight. Paula had wrapped herself in another blanket while she sat in a chair on the other side of the bars, and Ellen was glad that when Paula left, she had offered to leave it in the cell.

She heard footsteps, and Constable Wilson appeared at the bars. "Good morning. You have a visitor."

"Clarissa!" Ellen stood.

"I'll just need to inventory the things you've brought in, Ms. Simms. Back in a moment."

Clarissa reached through the bars to hug Ellen. "God. How are you?" She looked at the beds, the blankets. Her eyes settled on the toilet. "Not much privacy."

Ellen pointed over Clarissa's shoulder to the camera. "No privacy. Guard says it's okay to hold up a blanket."

"Damn, Ellen. You should not be in here."

Ellen shrugged. "It isn't so bad. The takeout dinner was alright, and Paula brought me some tea. She's very nice. She'll be back on the night shift."

"You'll be gone by then. You're not staying in here."

Constable Wilson appeared in the doorway. "These things are fine, Ms. Simms. Thank you for bringing them in. I'll close the door, to give you some privacy. Please remember the camera is up there, so you are both visible to the guard."

"Thanks," said Ellen, peering into the bag. "Toothpaste, soap—a towel! Bless you, Clarissa."

"Nonsense," said Clarissa. "I should have brought you a blow torch or something. Hand me one of those blankets."

Clarissa held the blanket up against the bars while Ellen washed. "You get any hot water out of that contraption, or just cold?"

"Just cold. But that's okay. There's a fountain too, and the water tastes not too bad." Ellen's voice was muffled as she peeled off her t-shirt. "Thanks for bringing a sweatshirt. It's cold in here. How's Monte?"

"He's good. Took him for a walk last night, and another one this morning. Ellen, there are reporters hanging around your place, asking stupid questions. I told them I'd sic Monte on them if they didn't leave me alone."

"You didn't!"

"I did. That kid next door, Jason, he told them, too. They were trying to get him to talk. He just kept saying, over and over, 'Mrs. Hoskins is the nicest lady in the world. Mrs. Hoskins is the nicest lady in the world.' Like a parrot. It was perfect."

Ellen flushed the toilet. "Thanks, Clarissa. You can put the blanket down now. Or use it to keep warm." She opened the toothpaste.

"Anyway, Jason asked if there was anything he could do and I said how about mowing the lawn. So he's getting right on it."

Ellen spat and rinsed. "He doesn't need to do that."

"Of course he does. He wants to help. Besides, you have gas powered lawn mower, and he figures the reporters will enjoy the noise."

"I'm sure they will." Ellen smiled. "Thanks so much, Clarissa."

"You're welcome. Does that camera record sound?"

"Just video."

"Good." Clarissa lowered her voice and pulled the chair close to the bars. "Sit. Pretend we're just having a nice pleasant chat, right?"

"What's up?"

"Act normal." Clarissa sat, then pulled the blanket over herself like a cloak. "I've got something to tell you."

Ellen laughed. "What's so mysterious?" She sat on the edge of the bunk and gathered the blankets. "You did tell them *everything* yesterday, didn't you?"

Clarissa nodded, exasperated. "Of course. Everything. Like, I wished Stan was out of your life, and I'm not sorry he's dead. And you're better off without him, but you didn't do it." She mimicked Jason. "Mrs. Hoskins is the nicest lady in the world."

Ellen laughed. "Then what's the big secret?"

"Okay. I'm sleeping on your couch, right?"

"Right. Oh, you mean last night? You stayed at my place again?"

"Yeah. I figured these jerks would let you go and I wanted to be there when you got home. Besides, Monte needed the company."

Ellen nodded. "I'm sure he appreciated it."

"Anyways, I'm sound asleep on the couch in your front room. It was stormy again, so there was lots of noise; wind, thunder, stuff. Anyway, I'm finally asleep, dead to the world, when suddenly Monte starts barking. Scares me half to death. So I sit up, and your front door is half open, and there's this guy standing there."

Ellen's eyes widened. "What?"

"That's just what I said. Actually, I said what the hell. Anyways, he sees me sit up on the couch, and he turns and runs. He's lucky you trained Monte to stay in the porch."

"Who was it?"

"Act normal!" Clarissa jerked her head back toward the camera. "I was wondering the same thing. He left his key in the door when he ran. Ellie, girl, you got something to tell me?"

Ellen stared at her blankly.

"Dish, girl. You got a boyfriend?"

"What?"

"I know I've seen him somewhere, but not in your living room, in the dark, at night. I can't place him. I was thinking he had something to do with where you work."

Ellen looked dazed. "Clarissa, I don't have a clue who you're talking about."

"Well, look. He's got a key to your front door and he's using it in the middle of the night. Either he's a boyfriend or…"

"Or what?"

"Or there's something else going on."

"Like what?"

Clarissa shrugged. "I don't know."

Ellen shook her head, slowly. "What did he look like?"

Clarissa frowned. "It was kinda dark. But he was fairly tall, slim. I thought late forties, early fifties, maybe younger. Grey hair, no beard, maybe a moustache. Glasses." She shook her head. "I know I've seen him somewhere. He's one of those people that you just know."

Ellen leaned back. "He doesn't sound like anybody I work with. Did you call the police?"

"Hell, no!" Clarissa shook her head. "Ellen, the guy had a key to your door. I figured I better talk to you first."

"He didn't get the key from me." Ellen's eyes widened. "Clarissa, remember I told you I found Stan's keys in the door?"

"Yeah. Oh, you think... God! Ellen, that would mean he's been in your place before!"

Ellen nodded. She suddenly felt even more chilled. "The blinds."

"The blinds?"

"The blinds. In my room. They were closed, that day. I usually leave them open."

"In your—" Clarissa lowered her voice. "In your bedroom?"

"Remember, I asked if you had been..."

Clarissa nodded. "Ellie, that was the day after Stan..."

After a quick knock, the metal door to the cell swung open. "Breakfast," said Constable Wilson, squatting to push a Styrofoam food container under the bars. "Fresh coffee's on its way. Will you take a cup now, Ms. Simms?"

Clarissa stared at her blankly.

"She'll have some, please," said Ellen. "We both take it black."

"Sugar?"

"No, thanks." Ellen waited until she had left. "Clarissa, we better tell them."

"You sure?"

"Of course I'm not sure. I'm not sure about anything anymore."

"What if…"

"What?" Ellen waited.

Clarissa finally leaned forward. "What if this just makes things worse?"

Ellen smiled glancing at the camera, the stained mattress, the toilet. "Things could be worse?"

Constable Wilson reappeared with two steaming Styrofoam cups. She balanced one cup carefully on the bottom rail of the door, and glanced down at the breakfast. "You really should eat that while it's hot, if you can. I'm afraid the food here doesn't improve with age."

Ellen bent to pick it up. "Thanks. Constable Wilson, Clarissa needs to tell you something."

Angie turned to face Clarissa, her eyebrows arching. Clarissa rolled her eyes at Ellen.

Ellen smiled. "No, no. She told you everything she knew yesterday. This is something new."

NINETEEN

ANGIE PULLED THE CRUISER in behind Clarissa's car. "Well, she seems to be waiting in her car, as asked." The small knot of reporters who were gathered behind the news van across from Ellen's house scurried over.

Harland stepped out onto the sidewalk and held up his hand. "Nothing to report," he said, waiting for Clarissa and Angie to enter the back yard. "The sergeant may have a statement for you later." Ignoring the babble of questions, he closed the gate and followed the women around to the side of the house.

Clarissa was unlocking the door, and Monte whined with excitement. "Good boy, Monte. Go out for a bit." She kicked off her sandals and turned to Angie. "Where do you want to start?"

"Mrs. Hoskins thought someone had been in the bedroom," said Angie. "I'll start there. Constable Harland, you check the porch."

"The porch?" Harland asked, incredulous.

"The porch," said Angie firmly. "Ms. Simms, you come with me."

Clarissa followed her. "I'm really not sure I'll know if anything's missing," she said.

Monte woofed, and Harland opened the door to let him in. He surveyed the porch. What the hell was wrong with Angie? She'd been snappish all the way over. Probably mad because the sergeant said Harland was to come along to search the house.

He opened a cabinet drawer, looked through the contents: two bags of dog treats, one package of small black bags. He read the label: *For picking up where your pet left off.* A spare leash. Some solution for washing dogs' ears. He lifted the drawer out, checked the cabinet behind it, then slid it back into place. Monte watched, wagging his tail. Harland reopened the drawer, pulled out a treat and tossed it to him.

The next drawer contained two pairs of gloves, one scarf and a hat, and a pair of those knitted things women wore on their legs for dance practice.

He imagined Ellen pulling on the leggings.

Hell's bells, he thought, checking behind the drawer and then slamming it closed. No wonder Angie wouldn't let him search the bedroom.

He turned his attention to the closet. A vacuum. A mop and a pail. Two brooms, one the old-fashioned straw kind like his mom used, the other fiber-bristled with a dust pan attached to the handle. On the shelf, a bottle of cleanser, half-used.

Monte settled against the door, rattling it in its frame. He should bring over some new weather-stripping, fix that for Ellen.

Three jackets hung from pegs on the wall. One was a quilted cotton plaid, a chore jacket like the kind his folks had on the farm. A pair of cotton gardening gloves protruded from the left pocket; in the pencil pocket was a narrow screwdriver.

The black wind-breaker next to it was most likely Stan's, and Harland checked the pockets. Empty. He reached for the beige raincoat.

"Bingo," called Angie. "John, we've got something."

She stood in the bedroom doorway, the small drawer from a night-stand in her hand. She held it up so he could see the back of it. "Lookee here."

Clarissa followed her into the kitchen. "What is it?"

Angie set the drawer on the table.

"Envelope." Harland pulled a small plastic bag from his pocket. Angie removed a pocket knife from its holster on her belt, and carefully slid its blade behind the envelope, working it under the strips of yellowed cellophane tape that held it to the drawer. The tape was no longer sticky, and seemed to hold the envelope in place out of habit. It fluttered away from the drawer and the envelope fell to the table.

Angie peered down at it. "Return address is Penticton Regional Hospital. Addressed to Miss E. White. Forwarded to Mrs. E. Hoskins, this address."

"White was Ellen's maiden name," said Clarissa.

Angie slid her knife under the envelope and flipped it over, then inserted the blade into the opening and twisted it sideways. Harland grasped the letter by its edge and slid it out. Angie used her knife again to unfold it. A photo fell out, the kind taken in booths in malls. Two teen-aged boys grinned cross-eyed at the camera. *"Dear Miss White, This photo was among Terry Walker's effects,"* Angie read. She looked at Clarissa.

"Terry Walker was driving the car Robbie died in."

"Robbie?"

"Ellen's brother. That's him, on the left. Fourteen, fifteen years ago, their car went off the highway out near Kaleden. No one knew why; animal on the road, driver error… cops never figured it out. Rolled down the bank and ended up on the tracks."

Angie winced. "I remember that one. I didn't make the connection with Ellen. Everyone was surprised the driver survived."

Clarissa nodded. "Terry was in a coma for ages."

Harland turned to her. "He died without coming out of it?"

"Yeah."

Angie sighed. "Actually, he did come out of it, briefly. His family were rushing to the hospital when he died."

"Really?" Clarissa looked up from the photo strip. "You mean, he was in a coma all that time and then came out of it, and then he *died?*"

"He was thrashing around, delirious. They gave him some medication to calm him, and he had an allergic reaction. He'd already been through so much. Within a few minutes, he was gone."

"My god, I never knew." Clarissa shook her head. "His poor family."

Harland pictured a young Ellen, grieving the loss of her brother. "So no one knows how the accident happened."

Angie pointed to the date on the letter. "This was written just after Terry died. Where was I… *among Terry Walker's effects. The family thought you might like to have it. Mrs. Walker tells me her son kept it in his wallet and that he thought highly of your brother.*

"*I am sorry to bother you during this time of loss. I know that the pain of losing your brother is still very fresh. However, you may be able to help me with something. His parents couldn't make sense of it, but I cannot get past the feeling that it was somehow important.*

"*During Terry's brief time of consciousness, he was very agitated. He may have been reliving the moments before the accident. He called out your brother's name, along with what sounded to me like 'Pooh Bear'. If this means anything to you, could you please contact me? Again, I am truly sorry for—*"

"Pete!" Clarissa slapped her forehead. "Oh, my god, of course! Pete Barry! That was who was in here last night."

"Pete Barry?" Angie looked at her.

"Yeah. I'd just seen him a couple weeks ago at Jugs, some stag party, I think."

"What does he have to do with…"

"He left Jugs in a huff when Stan called him Pooh Bear. I remember it was some kind of high school nick-name… the track team called him that."

Angie looked at Clarissa. "You don't mean *the* Pete Barry."

Harland whistled.

Clarissa nodded. *"The* Pete Barry, champion of all noble causes and manager of PenWest."

ANGIE CHECKED OVER HER SHOULDER and pulled away from the curb.

Harland turned to her. "Well?"

"Well. Let's see what Mr. Barry has to say for himself."

"It doesn't really make any sense, you know."

Angie grinned. "You don't think Hoskins could have been blackmailing him?"

"Barry's what, three, four years younger than Hoskins. And I don't picture Hoskins ever having been an athlete."

"But Clarissa was on the track team with Robbie, and she said Ellen knew the track team. She'd have known that this Pooh Bear thing the nurse wrote her about must have had something to do with Pete Barry."

Harland's neck colored. "Are you suggesting Ellen blackmailed Barry?"

"Maybe." Angie signaled left and slowed, waiting for traffic to clear. She glanced at Harland. "Probably not. But if she opened the letter, she might have told Hoskins."

"What do you mean, *if* she opened the letter. You think Hoskins opened her mail?"

Angie swore under her breath as an oncoming car ran the

amber. "What I'm saying, John, is that Ellen might never have gotten the letter. Think about it. There's that photo of Robbie. Call me a sentimental fool, but if it was my brother his photo wouldn't be taped to the back of a drawer."

"Maybe."

"On the other hand, I've never lost anyone like Ellen has. Maybe it was all too painful and she tucked it away and didn't think of it again."

"Tucked it away, maybe, but would you have taped it to the back of a drawer?"

"Probably not. But then, I wouldn't have lived with a man like Stan Hoskins. Maybe it was hidden *from* him."

Harland nodded slowly. He tried to form a picture in his mind, Ellen Hoskins approaching Pete Barry, coercing him into hiring her husband.

"Angie, Pete couldn't have been manager of PenWest fourteen years ago."

"No. But his daddy owned the place. Barry senior died about eight years ago, left it to his wife. That's the second wife, nice young thing but no head for business. So she cut a deal with young Pete. He manages it, makes her good money, gets it when she dies."

"Looks like he's doing alright." The curving driveway led through manicured grounds. "Pretty nice mansion."

"Pete's wife has money, too." Angie pulled to a stop, while Harland radioed in their location. "Her father's Marcus Alby, the politician that keeps getting re-elected because of his hard-line stance against youth crime."

The door opened before they could knock, and Pete Barry stepped outside. He was tall and slim, and Harland was surprised to see that his hair was completely gray. It was hard to imagine that this man was about the same age as Ellen.

"Can we do this outside? My wife is home."

Angie held out her card. "Of course. I'm Constable Wilson; we spoke on the phone. This is Constable John Harland."

Pete Barry's hand was shaky, but his grip was firm. He indicated a small gazebo. "We should be comfortable there. I can bring out some drinks if you'd like."

"No thank you," said Angie. "We only need a few moments of your time."

Barry pulled a handkerchief from his pocket and swept a few dried leaves from two of the wooden chairs that lined the gazebo. "We just returned from a trip. Haven't tidied up yet. Sorry." He pulled another chair over. "What's this about?"

"Well, as I said on the phone, we need to ask you a few questions about a former employee at your plant. What can you tell us about Mr. Stan Hoskins?"

Barry's hands clenched tight on his knees, the knuckles whitening. "I heard he was found dead."

"That's right." Angie waited.

Barry's eyes widened. "You don't think I... Oh, my god. Should I be calling a lawyer?"

Angie smiled. "That's entirely up to you, Mr. Barry."

Barry stood and paced across the gazebo.

Harland shifted in his chair. "Nice view of the lake you have here."

Barry blinked, then nodded absently.

"Mr. Barry, have you ever met Mr. Hoskins' wife?" Harland ignored Angie's warning look. "Ellen?"

"His... oh. Yes. I think I actually went to school with her. I was on the track team with... with her brother."

He sagged against the wall. "God. Her brother."

Angie stood. "Mr. Barry. What happened to Robbie White?"

"We were... Christ. We were kids. Racing to Kaleden. We did it two, three times before. Kids. Passing on the double solid, stupid risks. You know how it is. You're eighteen, you're invincible."

Harland glanced at Angie, who waited.

"I don't actually know how it happened, exactly. I passed them. Terry pulled out to pass me, but pulled back

in behind me instead. Maybe he missed a gear. Then he
pulled out again. I've never been clear on what happened.
Gravel on the road, maybe, or… they never found anything
wrong with the car. Anyway, it was on a corner." Barry
closed his eyes. "If Terry'd just pulled back in again, they
should've caught up on the straight stretch. By the time I
turned around and went back, there was a transport
stopped and the trucker was on his radio. I helped him put
up flares, and then… I left."

"Who knew about your involvement?" Angie asked.

"Stan. Stan Hoskins. Came to me about a week after
Terry died. Told me I'd go to jail for what I did—racing,
and then not coming forward. Showed me a letter from
Terry's nurse at the hospital, told me if I didn't get the old
man to give him a job, he'd go to the cops."

"Did Mrs. Hoskins know?"

"Mrs…. no. No, I… I don't think so. I only saw her
once or twice after that, but she treated me the same as
always." Barry ran his hand over his hair. "Look, Stan's
been blackmailing me for years. First it was just for the job,
then a couple weeks ago he came to me wanting cash."

Angie raised her chin. "So what did you do about it?"

"Do?" Barry looked at her. "I put him off for a bit. If I
started giving him cash, there'd be no end to it. But he had
me. I paid him a little, tried to buy some time while I figured out what to do. Christ, he was a pain in the ass. Never
thought I'd see the last of him."

"And now you have."

Barry glared at her. "I didn't kill him."

Angie stood. "Look, Pete. We've got a murder on our
hands, and you've got quite the motive. Why were you in
his house?"

Barry sighed. "So she saw me. I thought she was in
jail." He shook his head. "I should have known she'd be
out in no time. She was a mouse in high school. Wouldn't
hurt a fly. But I thought she'd at least be in for the night."

"Why were you there?"

"To get the letter. The one Stan had shown me. When I heard he'd been murdered, I figured it'd give me a motive. It did, didn't it? That's why you're here."

"How did you get in?"

"Stan left his keys on my desk last time he dropped by to threaten me." Barry looked up at the ceiling. "I saw the opportunity. I took it."

"You left the keys in the door the first time."

"The first... yes. Figured Stan'd just think that's where he'd left them."

Angie folded her arms across her chest. "You'd had one cut, then?"

"I... yes. I'd had one cut. Stan was getting louder, wanting money. I wanted him off my back. I thought I'd be able to... I just wanted that letter."

"That's unlawful entry. Two counts."

"Yes. I... I had to stop him. But I didn't kill him." Barry turned to Harland. "I didn't kill him."

Harland sighed, looked up at Angie.

Angie nodded. "Well, Mr. Barry. We have a problem. Hoskins is dead. You've got a motive. And there are those two counts of break and enter. You'll need to come downtown with us. And it would be a good idea to call that lawyer."

Barry looked stricken. He glanced toward the house. "But my... my wife."

Harland stood. "Let your wife know you're helping us with something regarding an employee. Let's keep this easy."

Barry nodded. He pulled a cell phone from his pocket, slowly punched in some numbers. "Honey? I'm going downtown with... yes. Just routine business. I'll tell you about it when I get home."

MACGREGOR SHOOK HIS HEAD. "I don't get it. Pete Barry? He's on all those committees, lobbying for his father-in-law. Get rid of protection for juveniles, bring in stricter laws for young drivers, harsher penalties. Mister time-to-get-tough-on-punk-crime himself."

Harland glanced at Angie and said nothing.

Angie was matter of fact. "I'm sorry, sir. I know he's a friend of yours."

"Yeah. Well. Mostly I just knew him on a business level, but... Just goes to know you never really know. Street racing, avoiding arrest." Macgregor shook his head.

"He was pretty young at the time."

"Yeah, but he's an adult now. This is illegal entry, at the least."

"Mrs. Hoskins isn't interested in pressing charges." Angie shrugged. "She was actually relieved to find out what was going on with the keys, and why someone had been in her house before, which, by the way, he admitted. Makes sense Barry figured he'd try to get the letter before Hoskins ruined him, and wanted to find it before his widow came across it packing his stuff. Couldn't risk the publicity."

"Would have been bad for his father-in-law, too. Think he had anything to do with Hoskins' death?"

Harland shook his head. "Not likely. Our money is on Franco. Simms put him at the scene, and he matches the description we got from Speare. Barry doesn't. Plus, Simms' ashtray, the one the dogs sniffed out? She swears it went missing around the time Stan disappeared. It turned up in the bushes beside her place with a fresh weld in it. Lab's checking it against the materials from Franco's shop."

"Franco?" Macgregor looked at Angie.

"Still on the loose. The bikes in his basement were the stolen ones, although the ones in his shop were legit." Angie grinned. "If he's dumb enough to weld a murder weapon back together just to try to frame somebody else, he won't be able to hide for long. Plus he'd be better off turning himself in than facing Helmet and his buddies. If he's got any brains at all he'll seek protective custody."

Harland frowned. "If he's the one that clobbered Stan with the ashtray, why wouldn't he just get rid of it? Why fix it, why put it back?"

Angie grinned. "Maybe because he's got the hots for its owner?"

"Still," Harland shook his head. "Pretty dumb for any guy to put everything on the line over…"

"Really."

"All the weld means is that he picked up the broken ashtray, put it back together and returned it to its owner. Pretty circumstantial. And hey, maybe it wasn't the murder weapon; maybe Hoskins boosted it on his way by Clarissa's; bit of petty thievery just to assert himself. It'd be right up his alley, as it were."

"And then Franco, the hero, shows up in time to rescue the fair maiden's belongings?" Angie thought about it. "Nah, more likely it was her all along. She sees Stan heading for home, she grabs her own ashtray, and clobbers him."

"Doesn't jibe with what Speare saw, if we can give him any credibility at all. He was sure it was a man."

Macgregor sighed. "You two about done with the wild theories? I'd like to salvage what's left of my Saturday."

Angie frowned. "Barry could have hired somebody. Or he could even have followed Hoskins home himself that night, finished off what Franco started. According to both witnesses, Hoskins walked away from the initial assault."

"Staggered away," said Harland. "Already dying."

Angie shrugged. "And we only have Barry's word that Hoskins left the keys on his desk. He might have taken them from his pocket that night. If Barry thought Hoskins packed the letter around with him, that would explain why the wallet's missing."

Harland looked at her. "What?"

"Hoskins' wallet wasn't on his body. According to Clarissa Simms, he'd had it with him earlier that night. He paid for the gas at Summerland."

Macgregor sighed.

"She said he had his bank card," said Harland. "Did she see his wallet?"

Angie nodded. "I asked her this morning, while we were searching the house. He could have lost it on his way home, but you'd have to admit that's quite a coincidence. I suppose that what Speare saw might have been an ordinary, garden-variety mugging."

Harland flipped back through his coffee-stained notebook. "Didn't Speare say the Capulets took something from Hoskins? Yeah, here it is, the 'spoils of their act'…"

Angie frowned. "Would he have seen a wallet from that distance?"

Harland shrugged. "Maybe we should get him in here, see if he can ID either Franco or Barry."

Macgregor groaned. "Anyone else know about Barry's connection to this?"

"Pete's wife knows we were asking him questions about Hoskins; he was an employee at his firm. Ms. Simms and Mrs. Hoskins know it's more than that, but neither one of them is particularly chatty."

"Okay. Let me sit on this for…" The front door buzzer wailed, and MacGregor flicked the switch for the door camera. "Oh, hell. Harland, your guy is back."

Mr. Speare stood at the entry, hat in hand, his odd garments glistening with rain. MacGregor pressed the intercom button. "Yes?"

"A word, a word. I must have word with your master. Get thee hence at once, good sir, and fetch him hither!"

"Go deal with him," growled MacGregor.

Harland crossed to the door. "Mr. Shakespeare. How are you today?"

"Petruchio!" As Speare clasped Harland's hand, his smile faded. "Methinks I am mistaken. 'Tis brave Othello. Yet thou art pale, good Moor. Othello! Heed me well. Evil is afoot. Thou must needst stop it!"

Harland settled him into a chair in the examination room. "What is this all about, Mr. Shakespeare?"

Speare leaned forward. "I didst see fair Desdemona, and her lady Emilia, this noonday news."

"They were on the news?"

"Aye, sir, on the television. Valley news at noon. Channel one-twenty-six."

Angie set a cup of coffee in front each of them, along with the bowl of creamers and sugar packets. "Desdemona was on the television?"

"Aye. With Emilia. They didst exit her abode in your company, and make haste in your chariot."

Angie sat down. "Did you see Lady Macbeth?"

"Nay, nay. Once, I thought she was the Lady Macbeth. And before that, Cleopatra. But on this I was mistaken. Upon speaking with her, and knowing her to be in the company of Desdemona, I recognized my error and knew her at once to be Emilia."

"I see."

Speare rubbed his brow. "But wait. Perhaps she was Cleopatra. On the news, they said she was going to jail. For murder. That wouldn't be Emilia. Or Desdemona. But it is behavior befitting Cleopatra. And the Lady Macbeth." He slapped himself vigorously on the forehead. "Think, think, why can't I *think?*"

Angie put a soothing hand on his arm. "Mr. Shakespeare, you said you had something important to tell us?"

"Yes. Yes. You must release these women. They didn't do it." He drew himself up. "'Twas I that didst put the wretched rogue's remains into the pipe, where didst he drown." He stirred another creamer into his coffee, and another. "On the news, they said the corpse had plugged the storm drain and flooded that poor man's home. His dog was distraught. I'm sorry. I meant no harm. But I couldn't just leave the body there. I needed it. Who'd have thought they'd cover him in on a Saturday?"

Harland looked at Angie, who was staring at Speare.

"*You* put him in the pipe?"

"Yes. It took a bit of work. The earth had wanted him,

badly; almost swallowed him, it did. Must have caved on him when he fell in—just one small corner of his jacket remained above ground. And the pipe! It would not accept him. Oh, his feet and legs, they were nothing. But then I had to get his shoulders in, and they were too wide. Finally, I came upon the solution."

Speare stood, flinging one hand high in the air. "One arm down by his side, the other up over his head. Then his shoulders were at an angle, and so in he went. I pushed him down as far as I could, and it wasn't easy. That cement pipe clutched at his clothing, and I had to shove him in with mine own feet, pushing him until he was well hidden. I thought I could retrieve him the next night, after dark. It was near morning, you see. Almost light. I hardly had need of my torch. Too bad I hadn't realized sooner that the earth had not swallowed his ghost, but his body. A ghost I had no use for. How would one capture that, contain it, direct it to walk and wail as the ghost of, say, King Hamlet ought? Nay, just his body. I needed the body. Oh, I should have taken it home at once, and daylight be damned."

Angie glanced at Harland, who was writing furiously. "Mr. Shakespeare, what did you do with Mr. Hoskins' wallet?"

"His wallet?" Speare blinked at her, then shook his head. "I had no use for his wallet. Only his body."

Harland looked up from his notepad. "What did you need the body for?"

"Alas, poor Yorik." Speare sighed, tapping his skull.

Harland looked at him blankly.

"Hamlet," said Speare. "The grave-digger scene."

MACGREGOR GRUNTED, tossing the file back on his desk. "So we have two confessions and three motives. Great." He leaned back in his chair. "Angie, your instincts were right about the chop shop. What do you make of this mess?"

Angie looked up at the ceiling. "I'm inclined to believe

Speare. He's not entirely with us, and yet his story had details that he shouldn't have known. If he didn't put the body in the pipe, he must have watched."

"You think he watched the widow do it?"

Angie considered. "I don't think he'd lie. Why would he cover for her?"

"Well, if he isn't lying, the widow is. Why would *she* lie?"

"She thought she was protecting her friend, Clarissa."

Macgregor grunted again. "Harland. What do you think?"

Harland thought they should let him take Ellen home.

He shrugged. "I'm with Angie on this. Speare's story makes sense in a strange sort of way. Mrs. Hoskins said she'd killed her husband and buried the body. Obviously she didn't. Most likely she said that because she thought she needed to cover for her friend." Harland hoped the Sarge wouldn't have to press charges on that.

"Yeah. Well, we can't very well hold her while we're doing a psych assessment on your buddy Shakespeare." He sighed. "Okay. Release Mrs. Hoskins. Advise her to stay where we can find her. What about the wallet?"

"Speare said the assailant took more than one thing from Hoskins. We're thinking the pieces of the ashtray, but maybe the wallet, too. Could be it fell out of Hoskins' pocket in the ditch, or in the pipe. Maybe when Speare was pushing him in. And if it came out in the pipe, it could be anywhere in the storm sewer system by now. Could be Pete Barry got it, but I think that's a stretch. Sarge, I don't think he was anywhere near there that night. Speare's description sounds more like Franco. Barry says he was home in bed. We could question his wife, check his alibi."

Macgregor grunted. "Leave it until we get Franco in here. If this is Franco's work, Pete's whereabouts that night is a non-issue. He's already off the hook for going into Hoskins' place, thanks to the widow."

Angie nodded. "So, are we taking any action over his

involvement in that street-racing accident? Seems a shame to ruin a man's life over something dumb that happened when he was a kid."

"Not up to me to decide." He flipped open the file, tossed in the photo of Stan, and slapped it closed. "Crown'll have to sort it out. I'll be glad when this one's sewn up."

As Harland left the sergeant's office, Angie put her hand on his arm. "John, be careful... Oh, hell. What am I saying. You only live once. Go spring the lady." She was still watching him as he walked down the hall to lock-up, so he forced his feet to maintain a sedate stride.

TWENTY

HARLAND PULLED HIS CAR into the lane behind Ellen's house. Next door, a teen-aged boy held Monte's forepaws, turning him in a circle. "Who's that?"

"Jason, the boy I told you about," said Ellen. "He seems to be giving Monte dance lessons."

Harland smiled, moving the car forward alongside the back of Ellen's garden shed. Jason saw them and released Monte, who ran to the gate.

"Ellen!" Jason's face lit up. "Are you okay?"

"I'm fine, Jason." The dog leapt in circles as Ellen opened the gate. "Hello, boy. Oh, I'm so glad to see you, too." She straightened up. "Thanks for taking care of him, Jason."

"No problem. I've just had him for a couple of hours. Clarissa spent last night at your place, and she was planning to stay here until you got home but her boys came home early from camping because of the storm and she went to pick them up. Oh, and she said to tell you she's put in for a few days off from work so she could be there for you. Said she was going to bake you a pie with a file in it."

Harland held his hand out. "Jason, I'm John Harland."

Jason wiped his palm on his shirt, then shook Harland's hand. "Nice to meet you, sir."

"Any media out front?"

Jason shook his head. "They gave up. I better get back to my homework." He leapt over the fence. "See you soon."

Ellen unlocked the door and fetched a treat for Monte, who was still wriggling with excitement. "Calm down, silly," she said, stroking his ears. Looking up at Harland, she sobered.

"John, what will happen to Mr. Speare?"

Harland leaned against the back of the door, hands on his hips. "Ellen, don't you worry about him. And don't go making up some cock-eyed story to save his bacon."

Ellen sighed. "That wasn't just a story, John. It was the truth."

"Ellen, you were stressed out. You weren't thinking straight. Even Angie's figured out you were just protecting Clarissa."

"You know better."

"Prove it."

"John, please. I gave you my statement."

"Never got a chance to type it up, and now I'm not real sure what you said—other than would have liked to have killed him but actually didn't, and you buried him. That can't be right, though, since we found him in the pipe. So any reasonable person would have to wonder if you were even there that night."

"Didn't you record our conversation?"

Harland shook his head. "No, ma'am."

Ellen's brows knitted into a frown.

"You took notes."

"Those notes no longer exist."

"John Harland." Ellen's hands went to her hips. "Don't be destroying evidence to protect me."

Harland smiled. "Said evidence met with an unfortunate accident. Wiped out by half a cup of coffee."

"John! You could lose your job!"

"Nope. It was an accident. Wasn't even me, Scout's honor. Angie did it."

"She didn't!"

"She dumped the coffee all over my notebook. Misha, helpful soul that she is, cleaned up, tore out the pertinent pages and tried to spread them out to dry, but they were too far gone. They were falling to pieces in her hands, so she pitched them."

Ellen groaned. "You could all be in trouble."

"Like I said, it was an accident. No way Angie or Misha would do that on purpose."

Ellen frowned, shaking her head.

Harland folded his arms across his chest. "Ellen. Nobody else knows exactly what you told me. And nobody's going to throw the book at Speare. He'll be getting a psychiatric evaluation and some therapy. Unlikely he'll have to go to jail. Franco broke the ashtray over Stan's head; weapon matches the wound, lab confirms it was fixed at his place. Case closed." He smiled. "Let sleeping dogs lie. No good will be served by you becoming a martyr."

"But didn't Mr. Shakespeare—I mean Mr. Speare— didn't he tell them he had to dig Stan up?"

"Speare said that the earth swallowed the body, and he had pulled it back out. Sounded to me like Stan had caved in part of the wall on his way into the ditch. Ellen, please. Trust me on this. Unless the autopsy says otherwise, Franco killed Stan. Speare hid the body. You're not involved. Let it stay that way." He put his hand on the doorknob.

"John, where are my manners. I should ask you in."

He shook his head. "Not tonight Ellen." He smiled, opened the door. "I'll be on my way."

Rock music blared from next door, then quieted down to a low thrum. Standing in the doorway, Ellen looked up to Jason's window, and raised her hand to wave. Jason gestured to Harland, pointed toward the street.

"News van is back," said Harland. "I'll deal with

them." He crouched to pat Monte. "Take care of the lady, boy." He stood. "I'm sure Clarissa will be by to check on you, too."

"Thank you." Ellen held out her hand, and he took it, cupped it in both of his own, then forced himself to release it.

She stood framed in the doorway, watching him as he headed for the front yard. Another car was pulling up, and he recognized a reporter from the daily paper. A flurry of questions greeted Harland, and he held up his hand. "Clear out now, folks. We have our suspect in custody down at the station, and there'll be a media release on its way. I'm sure you'll want to grant the victim's widow a little privacy now."

GROANS OF DISAPPOINTMENT FOLLOWED the media crews into their vehicles; doors slammed, engines roared to life. Constable John Harland stood with his thumbs hooked into his belt, watching until they were gone. Then he headed for his car. Ellen watched him go, stoking Monte's silky head as the dog leaned protectively against her leg.

It was starting to rain, small drops that shimmered in the rosy glow of the setting sun, and Harland tilted his face up to the rain for a moment before opening the car door. Then he turned, and raised his hand toward Ellen as though... she smiled. As though he was tipping a ten-gallon hat.

Harland's car splashed up the alley. The rain came down faster, the sunshine intensified. Ellen gave in to the moment. Monte looked on, tail wagging, as she stepped barefoot onto the wet grass and threw her arms outward, face to the sky, spinning and twirling in the shimmering rain.

ABOUT THE AUTHOR

Dawn Renaud is a freelance editor and writer in Penticton, B.C., Canada. She grew up on an isolated ranch outside Lumby, where some of her best friends were books. Summer jobs took her to fishing resorts and a northern guiding outfit. Sucked into the vortex of home computing back when a 40-megabyte hard drive was considered impressive, she helped local business owners program their newfangled electronic cash registers. Gigs as a cellblock matron, teacher's aide, and assistant literacy coordinator gave her plenty more fodder for fiction, as did the research for hundreds of magazine stories.